THE RED GONDOLA
AND THE COVA

Patricia Crandall

Patricia Crandall

Published by:
HAVAH Publishing
Ashland, OH
Havahpublishing.com

Address all inquiries to:
Patricia Crandall
www.patriciacrandall.com
pcrandall123@yahoo.com

ISBN: 978-1-64751-002-2

Library of Congress Control Number: 2019918913

Editor and Interior Layout Design: Amy Rice
Cover Designer: Geremy Woods

Every attempt has been made to source properly all quotes.

Printed in the United States of America

First Edition

I dedicate this book to:
Richard Kelley

My Number One Fan Of:
The Dog Men

RIP
You are greatly missed!

and

Amy Rice
HAVAH Publishing

Patricia Crandall

Contents

After he forced Alex into the marble entry of the magnificent Scottish Villa, and left him squirming with Master, Cain returned to his blue Nissan van. A frayed envelope was wedged into the front door handle.

He tore the envelope open and hands shaking, removed a pencil scratched note. He read: *Cain and Amalia, I know what you're up to with these kids, and I want part of the action. I have many contacts. We'll make more money as a team than you're earning on your own, trying to keep your boss and his clients satisfied. Man, it's a wonder you haven't been wasted by now. I'll meet you in the ticket line for gondola rides at Storm Mountain State Park today at 3:00. If you don't agree with my proposal, I'll bring it all down on your whole operation. Can't wait to join the team. A good friend.*

Cain crumpled the note and shoved it into his backpack. The thought of being found out and spending years in prison obstructed his ability to think clearly. He climbed into the van. He would have to tell Master and Amalia that an outsider knew about their operation. His eyes were wide and panicked, and he broke into a sweat.

Chapter 1

The Gift

Nine-year-old Caroline Wilkes scooted off the floor of her multi-gabled house in Grayridge, New York. She looked hopelessly down at the scattered jigsaw puzzle pieces. The flat-end and corner pieces created a sturdy frame, but the rest--impossible! She would need her brother's help, but that would have to wait. David was playing a Wii game with friends who came to the party to help him celebrate his ninth-grade graduation.

The party seemed to go on forever. To make matters more unbearable, adults had taken over by drinking specialty beer and wine, munching on sushi, chicken wings, and pizza. Their antics were not kid-appropriate, and Caroline was astute in noticing what some kids would only see on smarmy soap operas.

Her friend Mavis' dad was acting funny with women again. *Who was he kidding? And he was her dad's boss at the car dealers. At least he isn't tickling me. Mavis gets embarrassed when he does that to her friends.* Luckily, Caroline had escaped his tickling rampages. She was thankful that her own father kept his distance when her friends were around.

Caroline stretched. She owed David a present. Her lips turned up smugly. *Got it! I'll go to Storm Mountain State Park and get a free ticket for a gondola ride to the alpine slide. That'll be David's gift. He'll say, "Cool, Caro."*

Her mother would throw a fit when she learned that Caroline left the party to go to the State Park. Mom often complained these days that a lot of 'bad stuff' had moved into their neighborhood. She had told her and David that Storm Mountain State Park was off limits, unless she went with them.

Caroline peeked into the screened-in porch where her mom was lying passed out on the couch. She wanted to kiss mom's cheek so bad and give her a hug, but the stench of beer made her gag. Her lips trembled. *I'll try harder to be good, and maybe mom will stop drinking.* It seemed that mom's bouts of drinking had increased recently, and Caroline, like many children, gave herself the brunt of responsibility for the behavioral changes in her mother.

With tears stinging her eyes, she threw open the side door and let it slam as she raced down the porch steps. She couldn't escape the thoughts of guilt fast enough.

She slipped past guests lounging on green lawn chairs next to the pool. She continued along the lawn, stopping to peek into the large white tent. Mr. Mack was kissing Mrs. Addeson. *Creepy*!

Adults sure are weird, Caroline thought as she trotted down the road and skipped along the sidewalk to Storm Mountain State Park. In her innocence, boys still had cooties and were to be avoided. Her mind wandered away from the misbehavior she had seen to solely focus on the task of grabbing a ticket to surprise David with when she returned.

*****

At the park, she went directly to the large out-building, which housed the red gondolas that ascended to the summit of Storm Mountain, depositing skiers and snowboarders in winter, alpine sliders in spring and summer, and leaf peepers in autumn. It continued downwards in a loop, encircling the alpine villages of Gable Woods, Fleming Falls, and Slide Hollow, returning to the point of entry. Storm Mountain State Park closed for repairs during mid-April and reopened on Memorial Day.

Today, to the first three hundred people, the State Park was giving away free tickets for a gondola ride to the alpine slide when the mountain reopened on Memorial Day.

Patricia Crandall

Caroline came to an abrupt stop. What she saw before her took her breath away. Standing behind a yellow barricade, was a long line of people. She thought she would breeze in and out of the park and be home to help her mother cut David's cake at five o'clock. Once she saw all the other people, with the same idea to receive the free ticket, she realized that she would be later than she planned. She could hear her mother chiming in her mind, bawling her out for disobeying such a simple directive.

She shrugged her shoulders and fell in line behind a tall, long-limbed man who looked to be in his twenties. His curly red hair was banded in a ponytail, and he wore a ripped Exit Zero tee shirt and a nose stud. Large hoops stretched his ears to an obscene size. He was staring vacantly ahead, then he turned and looked down at her.

She looked away and watched workers set up booths and work on the gondolas. Large noisy forklifts and cranes with baskets, lifted and hauled gondolas attaching them to their frames. She was relieved that the man didn't talk to her and became lost in her thoughts as she waited.

There was a tap on Caroline's shoulder. Fearing her brother and his friend had followed to torment her, she raised her head, prepared to have an argument. Instead, she stared into the dark, rheumy eyes of the homeless drifter, Bud

Phoenix, often seen on the streets of Grayridge, rummaging for cans and bottles in trash cans. She had never imagined talking to him, so she was surprised that he was in such close proximity.

Bud asked in a croaky voice, "Hey, young miss, are you gonna ride in one of those shiny gondolas when the park opens?" He reeked of nicotine; her nose assaulted by the stale acrid exhale that hit her in the face as he spoke.

The line moved forward, and so did Caroline. Soon, she would collect her ticket and be on her way home. She kept hoping that she would recognize someone from school, so she could stand with them, instead of alone. There was something eerie about being by yourself, surrounded by adults, at nine-years-old.

Bud jabbered, "I've ridden in gondolas at ski resorts in New York and Vermont. I used to be a lift operator. I'm applyin' for a job here, but I want to get my free ticket first. Maybe I'll see you at the festival on opening day. Are you coming to it?" She felt uncomfortable, as Stranger Danger advice rang through her mind. He wasn't quite a stranger, but he was strange.

The red-headed man pocketing his ticket poked Bud on the shoulder. "Leave her alone, man. Can't you see you're making the kid nervous?"

Caroline recoiled as the two men arguing over her drew stares from the crowd. Suddenly, Bud said, "Mr. deSantos, just the fella I'm looking for."

As the two drew off to the side, Bud snapped at Caroline, "Save my place in line!"

She watched as a brief exchange was made between the two men, with Bud doing most of the talking. At first, the man, who apparently was deSantos, shook his head fiercely, then after looking into Bud's resolute face, he reluctantly stuffed his hands in his pockets. Before he marched off, he looked intensely at Caroline, and not knowing why, she took a sudden intake of breath. Bud slid in behind Caroline and breathed down her neck without saying a word. She was relieved to be at the head of the line. Relief flooded her to know that once she had the ticket in hand, she could make her way home.

An unsmiling woman, with snake tattoos on her arms, and assorted body piercings, leaned out of the ticket booth. She thrust out her hand and gave Caroline a ticket.

"Thank you," Caroline said, grateful this ordeal was over. Her mom was right. The park had become a creepy place to visit. Oddly, she had the same feelings about the weird adults at David's party.

She tucked the ticket in her pocket, turned, and followed a rush of people leaving the park. She walked past workers packing up their equipment and headed toward a shortcut, through the woods, to the sidewalk and home. With luck, she would be home in time for the cake cutting, happy to give David his gift. Caroline began thinking about how unnerving the walk through the woods felt in her solitude.

She wasn't prepared for a quick sudden movement and shrank back when Bud's voice croaked, "Wait up! I've got soda in the cooler behind those trees." He pointed a stubby forefinger toward an isolated clump of pine trees. "Would you like a can of Pepsi? I've got potato chips, too, or how 'bout a peanut butter cup?"

With her heart pounding in her throat, her mind's eye wandered to her mom's warning, "Don't go anywhere with a stranger." Caroline broke into a run, down the path, to a copious patch of bristlecone pine trees and the sidewalk. She looked over her shoulder and felt a jolt when she saw a ticket to the gondola ride lying on the ground. *No, no, no.*

She felt in her empty pocket. The ticket lying on the ground must be hers. No way was she going back to pick it up. *That old geezer may still be around.* People might chatter that he was "a harmless old badger," but to Caroline, he seemed ominously sketchy, something out of nightmares.

All she knew for sure was she wanted distance between them.

She walked sluggishly to the sidewalk. Suddenly, with an urge to return to the party with a gift for her brother, she spun around and raced back. She leaned over to pick up the ticket. A gnarled hand gripped her arm.

Chapter 2

Impromptu Gondola Ride

Caroline attempted to scream, but her mouth and nose were covered, and she was unable to breathe. She could not stop Bud from pushing and dragging her to a pine-treed copse. Fear started to creep in, and her mind reeled, trying to figure out if she had seen or heard how to escape a situation like this. Her mind blank, she resorted to what came naturally.

She kicked and punched, finally nailing her abductor in the groin. She slid to the ground, scraping her knees. Bud's face twisted in pain, and he grabbed himself. She jumped up, and despite a searing pain in her right arm, she ran so fast down a familiar path that her lungs felt like they would burst. She thought to scream, but there was no one to hear.

A red gondola glistening, from recent polishing and repairs, loomed ahead. Caroline ducked beneath plastic yellow tape meant to keep people out and raced toward it. She pulled at the door handle, and it swung open. Bud panted behind her. As she climbed inside, he tugged at her legs. She clung to the steel bar on the door. He yanked her toward him, and her grip loosened. *Fight! This is happening, keep fighting!*

On the ground, a striped tiger cat hissed and meowed. The cat sank his teeth into Bud's calf. Bud let go of Caroline and gripped his bleeding leg. She dragged herself onto the floor of the gondola and looked over her shoulder at the cat. Even in her panic, she recognized the stray cat her family and neighbors had taken turns feeding. She named the cat Hopper, since at times he hopped like a rabbit.

The cat attacked Bud again, and Bud howled. "Let go of my leg, you dang cat!" His fist came down on its head. Caroline's attention turned from her safety to Hopper's.

"Hopper, come!" Caroline shouted, regretting leaving David's party to get him a free gondola ride ticket. He never expected a gift from his dorky sister. Now, she was in big trouble. Suddenly, she felt helpless!

Her eyes widened and panicked as Hopper leaped into the gondola. She banged the door shut, securing the lock. Bud lunged for the handle. She braced herself against the seat and closed her eyes, expecting the door to fly open.

After a strong vibration and a jerking motion, Caroline opened her eyes wide in terror as the gondola climbed up the mountain. She turned and looked out the back window. Bud grinned triumphantly at her from the platform, after setting the gondolas in motion. Her heart skipped a beat as she watched him climb into the fourth gondola and follow close behind. A gondola ride, under these circumstances, was not an exciting thing, it was downright petrifying.

*****

The red gondola hurtled over the summit of Storm Mountain and slowed to a jerking motion as it passed over an unloading platform. The door opened, and Caroline and Hopper darted from the cabin. They tore around the base of a great white rock jutting out from the mountain and disappeared.

A fourth gondola swayed and slowed at the platform. Bud clamored out and looked at the three worn paths leading toward the summit of the mountain. Catching a flash of navy blue out of the corner of his eye, he raced down the path taken by Caroline and Hopper.

Her chest burning, Caroline climbed a craggy embankment, Hopper keeping pace at her side. She reached the pinnacle and scrambled on her hands and knees across a narrow precipice. She looked straight down a shadowy, dark abyss. There was no way she could climb down that slippery slope.

"Back to the rock!" she whispered aggressively to Hopper.

She swayed dizzily, managing to keep her balance. She turned around, and her heart stopped.

Bud wiggled his stunted fingers at her. "Gotcha."

In this moment, Hopper was swift on his feet in defense of Caroline. He hissed and arched his back, ready to fight.

Bud's face darkened demonically. "Not again dratted cat!" He grabbed Hopper by the scruff of the neck and dangled him, meowing and spitting, over the ledge. "There'll be nothing left of you, worthless critter." He flung the cat over the edge into the warren below.

"Hopper!" Caroline's scream echoed down the mountain. Fear started to grow inside her, tangible and dark. If Bud would do this to the cat, what were his intentions with her?

Chapter 3

Missing

Cheryl Wilkes wrung her hands. "David! The party's over, everyone's gone, and I can't find your sister. It's getting late! I'm worried!" Her red hair, normally pinned in a ladylike bun, escaped in wild tendrils as she plucked at it. "Stop texting. Where can she be?"

David was sprawled on the couch texting his best friend, Kyle Gardner. He and Kyle both had a crush on Kim Mercedes, and they were trying to one-up each other as to whom she liked best. The lean, 5' 11" fifteen-year-old sat up and raised his arms above his head, stretching with a series of popping noises. At least his stupid graduation party was over. It was more for grown-ups anyway.

He cringed to think his mom got loopy and passed out on the couch in front of his friends. Even worse, his dad stood off to the side in a drugged haze, absent even though he was present. And now that his mom and dad were separated, he had to deal with two sets of their weird friends.

"Ma, I don't have a clue where Caro is. Last I saw her, she was in the den doin' a puzzle. To get her off my back, I promised to help her finish the puzzle later. She's a pain." He kept on texting. "She's probably in the treehouse. Check there."

Cheryl stared out the window with a distorted vision from drinking too much wine. Once again, she had broken the promise to herself, and her kids, to give it up. She sighed. She really must get help to quit drinking. She squinted at the backyard. There was no movement in the treehouse.

Without warning, she was transported in time, watching Riley meticulously build the elaborate structure for his beloved tomboy daughter. Those were idyllic days, when happiness reigned in the Wilkes household.

With a jolt back to reality, Cheryl said in an agitated voice, "Put that phone down, young man, and help me look for your sister. The first place I checked was the treehouse, and she's not there."

"She probably went off to chase chipmunks and squirrels for her cages. Like the time she found that mangy mutt and took him to Doc Cooney's office without telling anyone," David complained. "She was gone for hours, and we looked all over for her. She's crazy." David didn't want to be bothered by this nonsense. *Caroline was fine, what could have possibly happened?* He thought. *Maybe aliens abducted her, mom, if we're lucky.*

"The sun's going to set in an hour, and I want Caroline in the house before dark," Cheryl persisted.

David watched his mother pull on a pink wool sweater and nearly lose her balance.

"Ma, you're drunk," he protested.

Cheryl straightened up as she slipped into scruffy moccasins. "You go look by the gnarly tree she climbs at the frog pond. Check the tent and the pool area ... she could have fallen asleep on a lounge. I'll check the backyard again." She shook David's arm. "Get off your bum, David. Let's go."

*****

After an hour of searching, and with darkness ascending, there was no sign of Caroline. The police were called.

Sitting off by himself in one corner of the room, David stared at his mother sitting inert on the oversized couch in the family room. Towering before her, documenting physical descriptions and time related events on a notepad, was Sergeant Joe Dillon. David shrank into the cushions when his dad marched into the room, a fierce look on his ruggedly handsome face.

"What do you mean, Caroline's missing?" Riley Wilkes demanded.

Lieutenant Dillon reached out to shake Riley's hand. When Riley ignored the gesture, Lieutenant Dillon went on to explain the reason he had been called to the house. "Mr. Wilkes, I need to ask you and Mrs. Wilkes a few questions before we put out an Amber Alert."

"An Amber Alert!" Riley's eyes grew big. He jabbed a finger at his soon to be ex-wife. "It's all her fault. When I left the house, she was stone cold drunk on the couch. Most likely, Caroline went off to a friend's house to get away from her drunken mother. She's done that before."

David held his breath and swiveled his head to his mom. Cheryl yelled, "Always the judge, Riley. And what were you smoking at the party?"

David clapped his hands over his ears. Scream, blame, and yell. That's all they did. *When did loving each other stop?*

Lieutenant Dillon nodded at him from across the room. David recovered when the detective winked and took charge. Somebody had to take charge. If things were left to his parents, Lieutenant Dillon would know more than he wanted about the Wilkes dirty laundry, and Caroline would still be missing.

While Lieutenant Dillon asked his mom and dad questions, David willed himself to imagine where Caro could have gone. *What would take her away from the party? She looked forward to doing the puzzle afterwards.* He felt bad calling her crazy.

Think David. She said something to him and Kyle while they played the X-box game. He was too involved in the game to remember what she said before she left the room. He texted Kyle.

Seconds later, there was a ping on his iPhone. He read Kyle's message: "Caroline said, 'I'm going to take a hop-skip to the village. I'll be back to help mom serve your cake.'" *That was eons ago. Where would a hop-skip to the village take her?*

David waited until Lieutenant Dillon ended the interview and prepared to leave. While his parents were still arguing in low voices, he scurried over to the lawman and tugged at his sleeve, "I think I know where Caro went, but I don't know why she hasn't come home."

Chapter 4

The Farmhouse

The thought of Hopper lying broken and gasping for a last breath immobilized Caroline. Unable to help herself she sobbed. Caroline had loved the tiger, but she hadn't imagined that he would try to protect her someday. Having seen him fighting for her made her that much more sentimental.

Bud shook her arm. "Be still! There'll be no hysterics."

Unable to get Hopper off her mind, Caroline wiped her sour mouth on the back of her hand. She felt swamped by dizziness, and it seemed like an eternity passed before she removed her wet hands from her face. When she did, she could not believe what she was seeing.

On the ledge, arguing with Bud, was the red-headed man with extended ear lobes last seen in the waiting line for a free gondola ticket. She flinched when Bud raised his voice, "Here's the goods, Cain. I want cash." He grinned viciously. Bud's appearance warped right in front of her. She was still trying to decipher what was happening right now.

Cain huffed at Bud. "One thing I don't understand, why didn't you contact Master directly? And who requested the girl? We have so many to choose from. Why this particular one?"

Bud put his hand on Cain's arm and felt him tense. "I don't need contact with Master, as long as you do my bidding. And I'm not ready to divulge the name of the person requesting Caroline. That person prefers to remain anonymous." He added with a trace of impatience, "You must warn Master, outsiders are aware of this club, and if they don't get a piece of the action, they'll talk. So will I." His smile was hard-edged, and he held out his hand. "Pay up."

Cain counted out bills and handed Bud a sizeable stack. Bud stuffed the money into a leather pouch. Then, taking a step backwards, he gave Caroline a weighty look before hastening away from the clearing.

*****

Cain looked hopelessly down at his Invicta Aviator watch and pulled out his iPhone. He texted furiously that he was running behind and prepared his cousin with the news that he would be bringing another girl back to the farmhouse.

An immediate response appeared on the phone telling him to come immediately. Master was due to arrive in half an hour. *"You better have a plausible explanation about this gatecrasher. We were explicitly told not to kidnap anymore kids. It appears the police, and Grayridge residents, are suspicious of several of our clients. And who is Bud?"* The phone blinked off.

Cain said archly to Caroline, "Come on, we've a ways to go, and I'm behind schedule." He grumbled incoherently to himself as he led her down a dirt path, leaving the rocky surfaces and clamorous gondolas behind.

Caroline stopped suddenly and breathed heavily. "I don't want to go with you. I want to go home right now." In her mind, this tactic was enough for her needs.

A flash of red darkened Cain's face. He reached out and yanked her arm, careful not to leave any marks. "You don't have a choice, girl. Get those feet moving, and keep your mouth shut, or I'll cut your tongue out."

As Caroline hobbled behind Cain, she imagined her mother frantically looking for her. With a tug on her heart, she knew David would search for her. Her dad would look for her only to impress his friends. All he cared about was getting high. She hated him, and she hated these two men who had captured her.

They tread carefully through the bowels of the mountain, spreading open thick, tangled brush. They edged precariously down a vertical path, descending slowly, skidding and sliding along the steep terrain. Caroline's little legs were far shorter than the man's, so he pulled her along after him. The light shifted and the dense pine woods opened onto an isolated clearing. The land flattened at the base and they walked along a dirt road for a half a mile.

Posted *No Trespassing!* signs appeared on the boundary where a white clapboard farmhouse stood in the center of the property. The house was shuttered, and warning signs were nailed to the doors.

Caroline blinked. It was the same house she visited with her mom and David to buy raw honey, eggs, and maple syrup. Farmer Miller and his family lived there when she was a toddler. Presently, it was owned by Will Inglis.

Fear turned to hope. The Inglis farmhouse was only two miles to Grayridge and home.

Chapter 5

Little Alex

Caroline stared at a gray Mercedes Benz Town Car parked in the circular driveway. As dazed and weary as she was, she recognized the familiar silver-gray luxury vehicle. *What was Mr. Pasos doing here?*

Suddenly, Cain's hand was in her hair, yanking her ponytail. "Don't dawdle," he said. Grudgingly, she moved forward with her neck cranked at an awful angle by the hairpulling technique of Cain.

They trudged past the leaf-strewn front porch and went around to the side of the house. Cain nudged her toward a low slanted cellar door. "Go inside," he said threateningly.

Caroline froze, her skin crawling. She shook her head fiercely. *No, I can't go inside.*

Cain squeezed her arm until it hurt. She began to weep as he pulled open the creaky door and pressed her back with a firm hand. He pushed her down broken concrete steps leading into a dark, rat and spider infested cellar with an earthen floor.

They went through a splintered wooden door, and a sudden brightness hurt her eyes. A lamp was turned on, and its light filled the room. She rubbed her eyes and stared.

Several filthy mattresses were spread out on the bare floor. On one mattress, two round blue eyes and a pair of slanted brown eyes stared back at her.

Cain shoved Caroline. She stumbled and fell on the floor before two young girls huddled together. "Lily Moon and Ae Cha, this is Caroline. It would be a good idea if you three got acquainted. You will be spending a lot of time together."

He strutted over to a closed door, at the far end of the room, and thumped on the door. A synthetically blond woman, her thick body stuffed into a nurse's uniform, poked her head out. She glanced at Caroline and pulled Cain by the wrist into the room. The door slammed shut.

*****

While harsh words were muffled and keyed up voices became louder behind the closed door, Caroline took in her surroundings. The room was large with mismatched furniture dating back to the flower-power seventies. The fusty cold air smelled of urine and rotten food. She gagged with each breath and began to feel queasy. *What time is it now?*

Thoughts of Hopper lying dead, or seriously wounded, at the bottom of a ravine caused her to tear up. She shut out the image and turned to the girl with slanted eyes. She asked, "Are you Lily Moon?"

Nodding her head, the girl fingered a miraculous medal clasped around her neck and blessed herself. There was a surreal calmness in her demeanor as she set the medal back against her exposed skin.

"Why are we here?" Caroline whispered anxiously.

Ae Cha whined with a heavy accent, "All the people here are bad, bad people." She squeezed her eyes shut and rocked her frail body back and forth. "Bad men and bad women do bad, bad things to Ae Cha."

"I pray to the Blessed Mother to help me get out of here." Lily Moon's voice trembled.

"Pray Blessed Mother will help me get away." Ae Cha begged.

"How old are you Lily Moon?" Caroline's heart was racing. She had no frame of reference for Ae Cha's explanation of "bad, bad people," but it sounded severe by the broken tone in her voice.

"Eight."

"Ae Cha?" She looked at the girl whose lips repeated, "bad," stuck on the word like it was the only thing left in her vocabulary.

"I heard Amalia say she's six." Lily Moon offered. "She speaks little English. She's from Viet Nam."

"Six, eight, and I'm nine." Caroline mumbled. "What's happening here with these people and... Master?"

Lily Moon was about to answer when the door flew open, and three adults and a small boy, dressed in sateen navy pants and a white silk blouse, came into the room. The boy looked to be three or four-years-old. Bawdry red lipstick was smeared across his chubby face. His dimpled hands busily rubbed it off.

Amalia jerked the boy's hands downwards.

"Look what you've done, Alex." She looked at him hard. "Stand still! I've got to scrub your face, and don't do it again, or I'll whip you."

While Amalia ground the lipstick off Alex's scrunched up face, Cain and another man stood off to one side and spoke animatedly.

"Mr. Pasos!" Caroline jumped up and hurried over to him. Surely this kind, gentle man would help her. He owned the True Value Hardware store in downtown Grayridge. He always offered her a lollipop when she went in his store with her mom or dad.

"Mr. Pasos, please take me home. I don't want to be here." She searched his face for a friendly sign. She found no sign of familiarity in him, which further confused her young brain.

Blatantly ignored, she listened as Pasos said to Cain. "Don't worry about Bud Phoenix. Let him have his way... if he brings two more girls, like this one, we'll give him an edge... he's careful, and it's not likely he'll get caught. Besides, he's burned a lot of people. We'll use him and waste him. The police won't know where to look for his killer. He has enemies everywhere."

Caroline tugged at Pasos' sleeve. "Mr. Pasos! I want to go home. You're talking to a bad man. He won't let me go home!"

Pasos yanked his sleeve away and went on in an unrelenting voice, "Father Tulley will be pleased this new one's on the list. He's fantasized about her a long time."

Caroline's eyes locked with Huan Pasos'.

"Will you take me home?" She asked weakly.

Pasos turned to Amalia and Alex. "Is Sapphire ready?" Amalia handed Alex over to Pasos. He said, "Remember, your name is Sapphire. Say it for me!"

"Alex." The boy mumbled.

Pasos made a fist.

"Sapphire," Alex stuttered.

After Huan Pasos and Alex were gone, Caroline shuffled across the floor and dropped down on the mattress beside Lily Moon. She planted her elbows on her knees and buried her face in her hands. Shoulders heaving, she sobbed. It was the kind of cry lost people make when no one is around to hear their pain, the kind that exhausts the person sobbing, the kind that oftentimes is never heard by another human being and can't be understood until one must wail that way themselves.

Chapter 6

A Game of Cat and Mouse

Standing on the high peak of Storm Mountain, overlooking the town of Grayridge, neighboring his village of Radcliff, sixty-eight-year-old Lester Cranshaw adjusted his binoculars. He studied the workers preparing the cherry red gondolas for a seasonal journey up the mountain, to loop around a horseshoe turn at the peak, and travel downwards again. He guided the binoculars to the right of the panorama and zeroed in on the edge of the Inglis property, crowded with hemlocks and fir trees, and eastern white pines. The farmhouse had been vacant for some time as the owner, Will Inglis, sat in jail, due to his incarceration for his involvement with illegal dog fighting.

On recent daily walks, Lester noticed activity at the house and grounds. Strangers came and went, and kids stood motionless in the side yard. He scratched his head. *Now, that don't add up. Kids just standing around stock-still. What's going on?* He lifted his shoulder. *Per'ap, they're on a school tour and have to be quiet.* Something about their posture imprinted the sight on his mind.

Finally, the distant cables squeaked and groaned to shut-down mode, and there was blessed silence. The gondolas were ready for Memorial Day and its opening festivities. The workers, in bright yellow coveralls, packed away tools and equipment and drove off in jeeps, trucks, and motorcycles. The new vacancy of the landscape made the air thinner without the din of vehicles to mar the brilliant silence that was soon taken over by the sound of nature.

"Paddy!" Lester called. "Come on, girl. Time to head home. I've got to put a heat pack on my back. Arthritis is kicking up." He strained to hear his three-legged Pointer thrashing in the brush with her pup, Patches. He smiled at the memory of when he first learned Paddy was going to have pups. He had been shocked and displeased at the thought of raising more dogs after the trauma surrounding her pregnancy.

Ten-year-old Wyatt Deshane and eleven-year-old Hannah Forbes had uncovered the dark world of illegal dog fights when they trespassed at a Vermont farm and peeped through a barn window. And when Paddy turned up missing, there was no holding Lester back from investigating the situation, and the kids joined in. In the dead of night, after Wyatt, Hannah, and Lester were captured and held hostage at the Inglis farm, Wyatt escaped and saved the lives of his friends. The Dog Men Adventure drew Lester into a tempest of animal abuse, lawlessness, and kidnapping. He saved Paddy, but not without a horrific fight that resulted in him being hospitalized and cost Paddy her leg.

"Gettin' late," he yelled, eyeing the sun's low position in the blue sky, streaked with darkening clouds, wandering above the pines. He never ceased to be amazed at witnessing subtle changes as twilight entered the mountain.

He adjusted his backpack and made his way down a slanting, narrow path with the aid of a walking stick, the top shaped like a gnome, his friend and neighbor, Topper Bolton carved for him. "Paddy! Patches! Come."

His girls bounded toward him; their fur knotted with burs. Lester grimaced. *I'll be combing a mess of ticks out of fur before I can eat supper.* He blinked back his surprise as Paddy raced back and forth and then stopped and nudged his legs.

"You're needing me to follow you. What for?" He turned slowly to keep his balance and floundered through a thicket full of needle-like prickers, having a hard time keeping up with the dogs. They came out near a mossy tree stump. Paddy sat down, her tail wagging. Out of breath, Lester inhaled deeply. "Where'd he come from, Paddy?"

A grey tiger cat was lying motionless at the base of the stump. Lester held onto his back as he knelt on the hard ground. He gently placed his hand on the cat's belly, feeling a pulse.

"He's alive, but barely."

He wrapped the cat in a flannel shirt, that he removed from his backpack, and cradled the limp animal in his arms. *Big guy. Heavy! Must be going on eighteen pounds!* With difficulty, he stood up and panted, "Come on, girls. Dusk is coming on fast. We've got to get this critter help, pronto, if he's gonna make it. There's only one person I know who can save his hide."

*****

Mae Bolton clasped her hands together. "Well, come on in. What creature have you got there, Lester?"

"A cat," Lester said as he trailed Mae into the cavernous, old-fashioned kitchen with a sloping floor. "Paddy and her pup found him on our hike at Storm Mountain. I thought he was dead as a doornail, but he's breathin.' Take a look."

Mae shooed a white cat off a plush mat stretched over the gleaming, damp tile floor. A pail of sudsy water and a rag mop were handy nearby. She picked up the mat and brushed tufts of white fur into a trash bin. She placed it on a bassinet she used to groom her three cats, miniature bulldog, and two rabbits.

In the background, news was broadcast on a Boise radio. She lowered the volume, keen to listen to commentary, as they visited.

"Put him here," she pointed, and together, they lay the cat on the mat.

As they stretched him out, his body twitched, and his eyes remained unfocused. His tongue lolled out.

"Oh my," Mae said. She examined him with gentle hands. "Nothing seems to be broken. Apparently, he had the wind knocked out of him. Must have fallen quite a distance."

Lester removed a glass from a cupboard and filled it with cold water. He took a long swallow and refilled the glass. "Coulda been chasin' somethin,' or somethin' chased him, and he shot over a ledge." He nodded his head, pondering. "Strange place for a domestic cat to be – on top of the mountain. Usually, they don't stray from the lowlands. The girls found him in a wooded area, nestled against a tree stump. Coulda' dragged himself there after the fall and passed out."

Mae checked the cat's ears. "Ears need to be swabbed," she removed a Q-tip from her dog-eared black leather medicine bag. "He's a tiger cat. No collar. Claws are still in. I'd say he's a stray, but someone's feeding him well by the looks of that pear-shaped belly." She measured a dropper of one of her tonics and eased open the cat's mouth, releasing the serum. Then she cleaned any remaining scratches and wounds and put the supplies away.

After washing her hands, Mae nodded toward the floor and the ample space next to a heat register. "We don't want him to fall off the bassinet when he regains consciousness. Set him on the floor next to the heat register, after I put the mat down."

Lester performed the task and straightened up. "Ouch, blasted kink in my back," he complained.

"I'll give you a bottle of my liniment. Rub it on your sore muscles, and you'll get relief." She watched the cat close his eyes and draw in his tongue. Suddenly, the twitching stopped, and he snored.

"Coffee?" Mae asked.

Lester shook his head. "I've got to get these gals home and take ticks off 'em with your natural repellent. It works, b'gosh." He scratched his whiskers. "Besides, morning comes too soon, and I've double chores to do on my seven acres. Steve's away to help his ailing ma."

Mae's green eyes twinkled. "I'll have this cat purring like a kitten by the end of the week. And after swallowing some of my potions, he'll look and act like the king he is."

"Knew it," Lester admired his neighbor of many years. Mae's raven black hair was streaked with white. She wore it in a timeless bob, and her feet were planted firmly on the ground in red socks and work boots.

"How's the old man?" Lester asked.

Mae frowned. "Don't refer to my husband as 'old man.' Topper's doing as well as he can in the nursing home." She raised her eyes to the clock. "Time I clean up and go have dinner with him." Mae and Topper Bolton had been Lester's neighbors for many years. Due to his disabilities, Topper was placed in a nursing home.

"I'll pay him a visit." Lester tipped his hat.

"You've been saying that since he went in The Danforth." Mae scolded. "I'll tell him you were asking for him." Her eyes slanted. "But it's not the same as spending time with him." Lester felt a twinge of guilt and promised himself he would go soon. It was hard to visit those places, at least for Lester, because he had never imagined Topper in there, not with the way Mae cared for him and all the animals.

Suddenly, Mae turned up the volume of the radio. She pressed a finger to her lips as Lester drew near to listen to breaking news.

"Amber alert." The bulletin went on to state Caroline Wilkes was missing, adding to the count of four local children who had vanished from Grayridge and Radcliffe in a short period of time. The announcer gave the number of a tip line to call, in the event anyone had information concerning the abductions.

Mae wrung her hands. "I know the Wilkes family and Caroline. She's a dear. I must go to her mother."

Lester was fumbling his way out the door when he said, "Her brother, David, just started working for me at the farm."

Then to the dogs, "Paddy! Patches! Come."

Chapter 7
Witnesses

Mae went to the Wilkes' house and found well-meaning neighbors fluttering around, being more of a nuisance than helpful. She slowly inhaled a deep breath and took charge of the situation. Several of the curiosity seekers left in a huff. Only then was she able to make a cup of chamomile tea for Cheryl and give her a consoling hug.

Lester drove his battered pick-up truck to the police station. His nephew, Lieutenant Joe Dillon, had immediately formed a multi-jurisdictional task force in search of the missing children, including his office, the State Highway Patrol, the BCI and ICE. Cute Lexi Mathers sat at the front desk and gave him a frazzled smile.

"I'm sorry, Mr. Cranshaw, but Lieutenant Dillon's way too busy this morning to see you." She raised her hands indicating four fingers. "Four Grayridge kids are missing. How evil is this world?" Her body language spoke to her agitation and ability to still be professional.

Lester huffed into his beard. "Lexi, I'm on the task force to search for these kids, and I'm here to get my orders.

I'm heading straight to Dillon's office." He started to walk past her.

Lexi gave him a whatever sign by raising her two hands, swung back to a case history on her computer and began furiously typing.

Lester tramped down the long sterile corridor mumbling, "Crazy world. Terrorists burning France. French borders forced into lockdown. Cops are stalked and murdered. Missing and abused kids..." He bypassed an occupied interrogation room and shot through the door of his nephew's office. The space, the size of a walk-in closet, smelled of stale soup, damp jackets and gloves, and sweet sticky buns.

Young David Wilkes sat in a straight-backed chair in front of Dillon's paper littered desk. The boy's shoulders sagged as he listened to Dillon give details about the search while seated adjacent to him. His face was ashen white, as the realization set in that Caroline could be in trouble. He had expected that his little sister would have already been home from an adventure; he had never imagined that she wouldn't come home at all.

Lester looked at David and then at his nephew. "Please tell me there's been headway in finding the kids." Lester was asking the question rhetorically, because David's demeanor said it all. He was hoping that his nephew's answer would spark hope in the young boy.

Lieutenant Joe Dillon never found it necessary to call a relative anything other than their first name. His mother and Lester's sister, Minnie, was in jail as an accomplice to rob a bank, and his father was never a factor in his life. He practically raised himself, guided occasionally by four good-natured bachelor uncles. Lester was one of them. Their only sister repeatedly caused them grief until she landed in jail. These old farmers could have walked away from Dillon at any time. Each, in their own way, raised him proper and presently, with a beautiful, spirited wife, four precious children and a successful law enforcement career, he did not take his good fortune for granted.

Dillon made a zero with his thumb and forefinger. "Before I have a word, I want you to hear what David has to say. Move that pile of books and sit down." He gestured to the wooden chair in the corner that acted as an impromptu shelf.

Lester cleared the chair, gripped his hat and sat down.

David said in a shaky voice, "I'll be honest Mr. Cranshaw and Lieutenant Dillon, I never liked my sister. Caro's always been a pain in the neck. But…," and he put his head down on the desk and sobbed. Normal sibling angst was turning into an inner turmoil for David as the hours that Caroline had been missing mounted.

Lester leaned over and squeezed David's shoulder. "What you're saying expresses normal feelings between sisters and brothers, son. The important thing now is you realize that you always loved her, and don't take that for granted when we find her."

Dillon nodded. "Good advice, Lester. Now David, can you tell us anything that would help us find her? I sense you know something."

David tapped his feet on the chair rungs. "Like I told you before, I'll bet Caro left my party to go to Storm Mountain State Park to watch the work crew set up the gondolas. Ma doesn't think so, 'because she told us not to go there unless she's with us." A funny look came on David's face. "I know Caro sneaks over there after school to see how the job's coming along. She can't wait 'til Memorial Day, when she can take a gondola ride to the top of Storm Mountain and come down on the Alpine slide. I can't wait either." He caught himself, and his face crumpled.

Dillon said to Lester, "Now I want you to hear Cheryl Wilkes' statement. I wrote it down the day Caroline went missing." She said: *It makes perfect sense to me now. I should have thought of Storm Mountain State Park immediately. Caroline is fascinated with the gondolas. I just found out from a friend of mine that she sees Caroline going there almost every day after school. I didn't punish her before the party, but I sure as heck was going to deal with it afterwards. I had forbidden her and David to go there. It used to be a beautiful area, but it's been taken over by druggies and gangs. It's no place for a child to go alone.*

Lieutenant Dillon explained, "David's and Cheryl's statements tie in with the only clue we have from a ticket agent, who claims she gave a ticket to a young girl resembling Caroline Wilkes on the day she went missing. The agent complained about a man harassing the youngster. She told the man to stop or she would call the cops. She doesn't know what happened after that, because the booth became busy." Dillon crinkled his brow. "That was the last sighting of Caroline and this man. My man is at the park following up these leads."

"Any ideas Lester?" Dillon asked. "I'd like to prod your common sense. You're usually 'right on' in these matters."

Lester's eyes lit up, as he felt a jolt of remembrance, recalling looking down at the Inglis farm while walking with Paddy and Patches along the rim of the woods on Storm

Mountain. He had seen children standing stock-still in the barnyard. How unnatural it was not to see a kid jumping, hopping, skipping, or playing tag. Then there was the incident finding the injured cat.

"Dillon!" Lester said sharply. He related this news to his nephew, adding how he brought the cat to Mae Bolton for healing.

David's head jerked up. He and Dillon spoke at the same time. David's voice cut through Dillon's. "Caro is crazy about that cat. He's a stray, and the neighborhood feeds him. Caro says he's her pet. She even named him Hopper, 'cause he hops like a rabbit. I'll bet she was with him and got lost in the woods." His concern was now focused on his poor sister being cold and afraid in the woods, but that was easier to stomach than imagining someone taking her.

Dillon remarked, "There should be no activity at the Inglis farm since Will Inglis is in jail." He fixed his eyes on his uncle. "Let's roll."

"I'm coming too," David dashed in front of them to the door.

Chapter 8
Moved

After Huan Pasos and Alex headed to their rendezvous, Caroline sat up and rubbed the tears from her eyes. Blinking rapidly, fear surging through her, she sensed Amalia's cold, analytical eyes examining her closely. Caroline hadn't a violent bone in her body, but inside she wanted to get back at all the people she had seen making the decisions for the kids. She didn't need to have a complete understanding to know that these were the faces of evil. She balled her fists.

Amalia said with a covert smile, "You need to relax, Miss Caroline. A good wash up will do you good. I'll take you upstairs to shower after I finish work at the computer." Shrugging, she said, "Perhaps Master will be in a better mood now that he has a pretty new miss to offer his friend, who has been impossible to please lately." Humming a Fleetwood Mack song, she thought, *maybe Cain's right about Caroline and Bud. These new additions could work to our advantage.* Nevertheless, she was aware of the potential dangers that lie ahead. *The police are closing in, one wrong move… just one…*

Amalia shot a thumb backwards, toward the room where a computer was set up. She said to the girls, "Don't try anything funny while I'm working." She left the door open, and the squishy sounds of her crepe soled shoes travelled across the wood floor to a dented metal desk. She sat down, rolling to the desk.

While her concentration was on the pairing of each of the girls with clients, whose names raced boldly across the screen, occasionally she glanced at their forlorn faces and tense bodies perched on the edge of a filthy mattress. Amalia didn't feel the normal guilt that she had started with. The money was too good for that; she had become savage in her skills to make sure that she could save and squander as much money as possible, while the opportunity was still available. Never mind that she was always cooped up with her charges, leaving her unable to enjoy her spoils.

Caroline whispered to Lily Moon, "How long have you been here?"

Lily Moon grasped the miraculous medal hanging around her neck. Calm radiated from her as she rubbed the medal. "Couple of weeks! A man dressed as a clown stopped his car and called me over to see his dog dressed in a frilly collar. I went to the car. It was banged up, and another man pulled me inside. I screamed, but he put a gag in my mouth.

The smell and taste of the cloth were awful. I must have fallen asleep, 'cause when I woke up, I was here."

Caroline's eyes darted to Amalia, concentrating on the computer screen. She asked Ae Cha in a low voice, "How long have you been here?"

Ae Cha counted on her fingers. "Eight weeks. Mama sold me to a man for drugs. She won't take me back home, 'cause she wants drugs more than she wants me."

Caroline wanted her mom so much it hurt. *How could a mother sell her child for any reason?* She bit down on her lip, tasting blood. It raised questions, but she knew better. *Mom just has a drinking problem. She wouldn't do that.*

Lily Moon piped up, "Tell Caroline what happens when you and Alex are taken to Master's friends."

"Uh, nope." Ae Cha hugged her knees to her chest and rocked back and forth. The light in her eyes faded when pressed for information.

Lily Moon said urgently, "Tell her!" She looked anxiously at Amalia printing copies from the computer. "Amalia's almost finished with her work. She'll be here soon."

Ae Cha's eyes glazed over. "Uh, don't want to."

"You must tell her, Ae Cha," Lily Moon pleaded. "Caroline must know what's going on. Maybe she can help us get away from here."

Ae Cha swiped a finger beneath her nose, "Master's friends tell me I'm pretty, and I smell nice. They give me candy or a dish of ice cream afterwards."

"After what?" Caroline's voice raised an octave.

"After we play silly games on furry rugs, we move to a fancy bed with silk sheets and get bare-naked. It doesn't take long to *love*." Ae Cha's voice could scarcely be heard.

Lily Moon huffed, "Ae Cha, you give these people sex stuff, not *love*. There's a difference."

"What will we have to give them, Lily Moon?" Caroline felt prickles on her neck. She had heard the word, but she had no idea what that meant.

"Same thing." She fingered her miraculous medal.

*****

Suddenly a door burst open. Cain flew into the room, breathless. "Amalia?"

"I'm here, luv." Amalia slipped back into the room, closing the door behind her. "Cain, you're white as a sheet.

What's wrong?" Her playful demeanor changed as soon as she saw him.

Cain snapped a large green garbage open and began tossing in food and clothing. "We must leave at once."

Amalia looked at Cain like she thought he was an imbecile. "Are you out of your mind? Why?"

"A snitch gave away our location and exposed the human trafficking operation to the police! Master's here with orders." Cain was clearly not joking, but Amalia was still on a high from running the numbers and names and seeing the new income that could be made.

Amalia made a sound of annoyance. Before she could complain, the door pushed open and three men marched into the room, Huan Pesos, Marvin Patterson of Patterson Motors, and Reverend James Tulley, Pastor of Blessed Sacrament Church.

*****

The three men exchanged looks with Cain and Amalia. Huan Pesos spoke first, gruffly, "Take the kids to the old Boomhower cabin. Here's the directions." He handed Cain a printout sheet. There were no pleasantries on this visit.

"Shouldn't we get rid of evidence before we leave?" Amalia said shaken.

"Gather anything incriminating," Patterson snapped. "If you followed orders, there shouldn't be evidence. The police won't be able to prove anything by food scraps and wrappers. Homeless drifters could leave that trail behind." He eyed the sparse surroundings. "Take what you need and clear out."

"Who's the snitch?" Amalia asked, shoving clothing and blankets into a box. She grabbed her computer from the other room. The answer here could change the whole operation and could cost someone their life. Her biggest concern was that their newest accomplice had sold them out, and she had wanted to explore his usefulness.

Patterson glanced at his watch. "Just hightail it out of here. The police don't waste time. And there'll be FBI and immigration officials to fend off."

"I know who it is," Amalia lied. She was hoping for brownie points and a raise.

Pesos said in a sharp voice. "That knowledge doesn't bode well for you, Amalia. Must we deal with you too?"

Chapter 9

Trash Collectors

Grim faced, and with shivers of dread assailing them, Lester, Dillon, David, and a team of police technicians took in the waste strewn about the room in the bowels of the Inglis farm.

The lead tech ordered his men, "Bag all the evidence you find in every inch of this cellar."

Lester shoved his hands deep into his pockets as his eyes rolled over dirty mattresses spread on the floor. Food wrappers, plastic take-out containers, dirty socks and underwear had been tossed into a heap in one corner of the room. It was clear to him that there had been kids here. The underwear themselves were too small to have belonged to an adult, not to mention the designs were reminiscent of the packages hanging for sale in the little girl's aisle at the box stores.

"No signs of kids being here." One of the technicians reported. Lester cursed as technicians tagged and bagged evidence and sealed each individual plastic sack in containers. Other loose samples were being put into vials and photos were taken. The sense of urgency wasn't to his liking.

These were children they were looking for, that he had seen standing in the yard.

David accidentally kicked an empty can of SpaghettiOs across the room, creating a snap-popping noise. Several men reached for their guns. After seeing a tin can bouncing across the floor, everyone breathed easily, patted their holsters and resumed their tasks.

Dillon grabbed David's shoulder and ushered him toward the door. "Time to get some fresh air, buddy. I'll get written up, and a report sent to my superior, if any of these men complain that you're here. There'll be plenty for you to do later. Lester and I won't be long, I promise." He winked.

David shuffled toward the door and once outside, he welcomed the bracing air. He slumped down on the porch step, with his chin in his hands, and watched State Troopers, dogs, and investigators do their work. He wished for the day when he could become one of them. His passion to become a State Trooper was never as intense as it was now.

His eyes focused on the big red barns once filled with haybales and animals. The tractors and farm equipment were unnaturally silent. A few chickens pecked at food in the driveway. *The caretaker must be feeding the chickens. It sure as heck isn't Will Inglis. That dog abuser creep is in jail, thanks to Lester.*

David stiffened. *The caretaker must know if the kids were here.* He sat up. *Caro, where are you? Were you kept at this farm?* The thought bothered him. He needed to do something about it.

Inside the cellar, Dillon and Lester moved out of the way of the technicians. Dillon rubbed his lips and said, "We're dealing with a group linked to the national network of sex-traffickers serving clients in this area. There's a big picture unfolding. After we're done here, I'm going to see Will Inglis."

"You mean to tell me Inglis can work a trick from his jail cell? Don't wardens keep a tight watch on these guys? Or are they at a picnic, like it's rumored to be in jail." Lester looked disgusted.

"You'd be shocked by what occurs inside our prisons." Dillon investigated Lester's resolute face. In a voice laced with sarcasm, he said, "On the other hand, jail time can be downright frightening. Take your pick, old dad."

Lester grunted, "Something smells, and it ain't garbage. A sophisticated group like these child takers ain't gonna leave a trail behind to make it easy for the cops."

Dillon replied instantly. "We'll see what the lab reports. This could be trash from some homeless group or underage kids drinking and drugging. Whoever it is, and I'm going to bet it's the sex trafficking group with the kids, panicked and ran." He squinted his eyes, "Which means someone tipped them off. We've got a snitch to expose. Now, excuse me while I check with the techs, and we'll leave." Dillon didn't know he had anyone in his ranks he couldn't trust, but he was more bothered than ever. What they were dealing with was so ugly that a feeling human being couldn't look the other way, unless they were involved. It turned his stomach to think that there was someone around him involved in this fiasco.

As Dillon and Lester made their way through the labyrinth of a cellar to outdoors, Dillon said, "Meanwhile, I'm counting on you to come up with a place where these kids were taken, a place where the perverts feel safe."

When the door opened, Lester's eyes took in the vast fields abutting the mountains. "There are a gazillion vacated hunting lodges, camps, and summer homes where they could be. It'll be like finding a needle in a haystack." His mind started considering every nook and cranny of the mountain, he would have to take the dogs out to see if they caught onto something.

Dillon drew a deep breath. "You know these mountains, and the surrounding area, better than anyone I know. In the meantime, I've got to get David settled somewhere safe and comfortable. His mother is going into a rest home for long term care. She's had a mental collapse."

"What about his father?" Lester asked, already knowing the answer.

"What do you think?"

Lester spat on the ground. "David can stay with me."

Chapter 10
Too Ill to Run

Caroline felt dizzy and cold when she raised her head. Her whole body shivered.

The strange room she found herself in was pitch dark, and the acrid smell of garbage and damp earth burned her nostrils. Worse, were the unknown critters skittering close to her. She could hear them in the darkness, and she imagined that they were as large as they sounded to her little ears.

The last thing she remembered was Amalia forcing a cloth with a sickening odor over her mouth and nose. She gagged, and soon after, her mind became woolly. She recalled floating into the filthy van, being crushed between cardboard boxes filled with fancy dresses and shoes and Ae Cha and Lily Moon. During the short ride to their new destination, the van bumped and jostled upwards over steep, twisting and bumpy roads.

In her woozy state, Caroline managed to keep track of the distance and steep climb it took to go from one location to the other. She calculated this site was not far from the Inglis farm. They weren't in the vehicle for too long, so she found solace in that they couldn't have gone too far, meaning she could still get home.

How could this happen to me? In school, she and other students were subjected to lectures about strangers who threaten kids and force them into unimaginable situations. The speaker pressed hard upon the students to never go with a stranger. Scream, kick, do whatever is necessary to get someone's attention. She had followed the rules, and nothing worked. A kidnapper snatched her up effortlessly and brought her to a place with other captured kids. They all had been rendered helpless. It happened so fast; it was out of their control to help themselves.

Nothing bad took place yet. She knew it was a matter of time before someone would... she could feel the sweat forming on her skin as vivid dark images played in her mind.

Someone must be looking for her and the others to have chased these weirdos away from the Inglis farm. Soon, her mom and David would find her. She desperately needed to believe that. Clinging to hope helped a little.

*****

A body stirred on the army blanket stretched out on the cold floor next to Caroline. "Where are we?" Lily Moon yawned. She vigorously rubbed her numb fingers.

"Inside a smelly old camp," Caroline said miserably.

"I'm sick. My stomach hurts." Ae Cha whined. She lay on the blanket on the other side of Lily Moon. As she grabbed her stomach, Lily Moon skittered away from her, trying to keep away in case she was contagious.

"Lay still and rub your belly." Caroline coaxed. The room smelled ghastly, without adding vomit to the mix. "It's probably from the stuff Amalia pressed on your nose and mouth along with the jumbled ride. Just be still. You'll be okay in a while." Caroline slipped into the motherly role quite simply, being the oldest.

Lily Moon stood up unsteadily and supported her back against the bare wall. "Where's Amalia? Where's Cain?"

"Maybe they've gone and left us alone." Ae Cha's tepid voice was hopeful.

Caroline looked in Ae Cha's direction strangely. Her eyes were adjusting to the darkness, and she could see the girl's bunched shape on the floor. "Did they leave you alone before, Ae Cha?" This new revelation could make all the difference.

"Once," Ae Cha shook her head. "No, twice; for a long time, but Alex and I were chained to a wall, or our hands and feet were tied so we couldn't get away."

Caroline's tremulous voice said, "This time we're not chained to a wall or tied up." Her eyes became slits, "They don't seem to be here. It's too quiet." She rolled her legs off the blanket and stood up slowly. Waves of nausea came over her. She took deep breaths, and gradually, the queasiness went away. "Do you think it's a trap to see if we'll try to run away, Lily Moon?" Her mind was quick to play through the possible scenarios so when she did make a move, she would have a chance.

"No, I think they've gone somewhere, but not for long."

"Stay put," Caroline directed the girls. "I'm going to look around. If I'm caught, I'll be the one in trouble, not you two."

*****

Caroline wobbled across the bedroom floor and crept into the bare kitchen. There was a table and two chairs, nothing else. She eased her way around a wall, turned a corner, and mid-way down, there was a door. She leaned into the door and gripped the latch. She pushed, and the door opened.

Fresh air, with a biting chill, embraced her. It was pitch dark, and the moon was hidden by fast moving clouds.

At intervals, it peeked out, brightening the forest but not for long. Caroline's teeth chattered from the cold. The late spring air was about 52 degrees. All she had on was a long-sleeved cotton shirt and torn leggings. No matter. She was free, and there were no signs of Cain and Amalia.

"Lily Moon! Ae Cha! We can get away! Hurry!"

Lily Moon nearly knocked Caroline over as she rushed through the open door. Her willingness to escape motivated Caroline even more.

"Ae Cha!" Caroline called out, as loud as she dared.

Ae Cha sobbed. "I can't get up. My stomach hurts so bad. Don't leave me, Caroline. Lily Moon!" The alarm in her voice gave pause to the two potential escapees as they considered staying with Ae Cha.

Caroline hesitated, but not for long before calling over her shoulder, "Pray we can bring back help, Ae Cha." Then she sprinted down the gravel path and flew past Lily Moon into a fortress of pine trees. The two girls ran like they were being chased by demons.

*****

After stumbling over fallen logs and jutting rocks, Lily Moon panted at Caroline, "Can we take a break? We've gone a mile at least."

Caroline dropped to the ground and rolled over wet pine needles, leaves, and moss which clung to her clothes. Lying stretched out on the earthen floor, she blended in with the woodland. She flexed her deadened fingers and lowered her hand, snapping it back up.

"Yikes! What's this?" She shrieked and clapped her hands over her mouth.

A furry creature purred loudly, and a fluffy tail swished back and forth.

"Hopper!" Caroline whispered hoarsely. Clumsily, she raised her pet to her chest and hugged him. "I thought you were dead!" She nuzzled her face into his clean smelling fur, rocking him back and forth. "Where did you come from? Oh, I wish you could talk." Caroline was oblivious to the tears of joy that had slipped down her cheeks.

Lily Moon gave Caroline a jaw dropping stare. "Is this your cat?" She squatted down, attempting to stay off the damp ground. She reached out and touched Hopper's groomed fur.

Tears spilled down Caroline's cheeks. She released Hopper to the ground, brushed herself off, and stood up. "I don't know how Hopper got here, but it's a miracle he's alive. The last time I saw him he was flung over a ledge by Bud Phoenix."

"Look, he's going away." Lily Moon pointed to Hopper swaggering down a path. His bushy tail seemed to beckon the girls to follow him in his confident gait.

"And we're following him. We don't have a clue as to where we're going." Caroline said breathlessly. "Maybe he'll lead us home." She crossed her fingers behind her back. He had found her the first time when she had needed him.

Chapter 11

Finding Alex

There was a sharp intake of breath, and Amalia pointed, "Look! The back door's wide open! Those kids are gone in a heartbeat."

With no electricity in the cold, dark house, she flicked on a Navy Seal LED flashlight. It lit up the large, old fashioned kitchen like daylight had entered. She tore into the bedroom and waved the light across the room. "I found one," she yelled, running over to Ae Cha, scrunched up on a moldy blanket, vomiting on the floor.

Amalia whipped Ae Cha's head up and pressed it between her hands. "Where are Caroline and Lily Moon?"

Ae Cha fluttered her hand toward the door between retching.

Amalia gave Cain a withering look. "They're gone."

He went over to Ae Cha and knelt, touching her skin. "She's burning up." He stood up, wiped his hands on his pants and headed toward the door. This was as much trouble as the cops coming—a sick child and two missing. Master would have their heads.

Amalia glared devil's eyes at her cousin. "Where are you going?"

"To the truck to get cell phone reception. We need to get Doc Jewel here, pronto, to examine Ae Cha, before we have another corpse on our hands. And with the other two gone, I'll tell her to bring the search dogs."

Contemplating what went wrong, he scratched his head. The girls should have been knocked out cold, after Amalia gave them a sedative when they first arrived here. He and Amalia were only gone fifteen minutes to turn the truck's motor on for warmth and to take a snort. Unless...

"Amalia, what sedative did you give the girls?"

"Valium."

"What dosage?"

"2.5 mg."

"Damn! You should have given them 6.5 mg of Ambien."

"Cain! We want to sedate them, not give them an overdose."

He ground his teeth. Due to the miscalculations, they would pay dearly. Master will be enraged. He shuffled his feet. "While I'm making calls, you go outside and try to find Caroline and Lily Moon. They can't have gone too far. It's cold and wet out there, and they don't have a clue where they are. This place is miles from town."

Amalia shoved bottled water and a flashlight into a backpack. "It's three-quarters of a mile to the Inglis farm," she reminded him. "If they make their way to that farm, we're doomed." She hesitated, "You said you're making calls...to whom, besides Doc Jewel?" She looked at him suspiciously.

When he did not answer, she said accusingly, "You're not going to tell Master about this, are you Cain?" She was still invested in this venture and did not want their negligence to bar them from future profits.

"Bring the girls back, and our problem is solved." He went out the door. He knew he would have to tell, sooner rather than later, because Master was too involved. These assets were too valuable to risk leaving Master out of the loop for too long. He was quick to eliminate sloppy operators.

*****

Outside, Amalia stood in the dark and flashed the light, looking right and left. *Now, if I were a kid running from thugs, what path would I take?* She zipped her jacket up to her neck and went down to the tree-lined path and turned north.

Amalia swung the powerful flashlight back and forth, catching every creature, stone, leaf, and fallen tree limb in its path.

Meanwhile, Caroline, Lily Moon, and Hopper plodded on about a mile and a half ahead. Lily Moon clung to the back of Caroline's tee-shirt to help guide her steps in the dark. At times, it was pitch black, and they could see nothing at all. Exhausted, cold, and beyond hungry, they forged ahead. The knowledge that they would soon be missed and followed remained at the forefront of their fledgling minds.

Suddenly, the moon broke through the clouds and Caroline's heart froze. In the middle of a copse of tall pines, amassed in a pyre were small skeletons. On top of the funeral pile lay one tiny body. Dressed in poetic clothes and a velvet coat, Alex lay on his back, his flesh-eaten hands and arms crossed over his chest. The bruising on his face and neck exposed bite marks and horrors that only the little boy knew existed.

Lily Moon coughed and sobbed at the same time. She could barely get the name out. "Alex?" Seeing him for the first time since he had left the farmhouse, Lily Moon didn't know how to process his lifeless body.

Caroline felt terror like none other she had experienced. "We're out of here! Hopper, come!" She wanted to put as much distance as possible between this funeral pyre and herself. This was a place of nightmares.

Hopper trotted on, leading the way away from Alex and the other lifeless bodies. *Where did they all come from?* Caroline shook her head to push the thought out of her mind. It wasn't going to aid their escape to try to puzzle out what was going on. She would have to leave that to the authorities once she was safe,

Caroline, grim-faced, and Lily Moon, sobbing noisily, still out of control, followed Hopper through the dense woods, constantly looking over their shoulders.

"Shhh," Caroline stopped in her tracks and placed her finger on her lips. "Be quiet. I hear something." Her heart started to race as she stared into the darkness waiting for the sound to come again.

Some distance away a voice screeched, "Lily Moon, Caroline, I know you're here. Come to me, now!"

The girls hunched down between a boulder and low-hanging branches, which clawed at their faces, necks, and hands, leaving scratches that bled. They were unaware of the damage to their bodies as they desperately tried to hide from Amalia.

A bright light circled them as Amalia crashed through the woods screaming their names.

With her heart beating *whoosh, whoosh, whoosh*, Caroline threw herself on top of Lily Moon. Her own clothes were muddied and dark, blending in with the mountain. Lily Moon's sweatshirt was pure white.

Amalia's heavy tread crunched along the path and stopped. Her high-pitched voice threatened, "It's only a matter of time before we find you. Soon, we'll have killer dogs searching for you. I guarantee Hannibal and Caesar will rip you apart. Best you come with me before that happens."

Caroline could feel Lily Moon quivering beneath her. Amalia's threats always came true. Lily Moon considered giving up her position, and had she not had Caroline parked on top of her, she may have surrendered to forgo the consequence of the dogs.

The light from the flashlight swung back and forth, glancing over Caroline's muddied back, then receded.

Amalia headed on, shouting until her voice trailed in the distance. "Lily Moon and Caroline, there'll be no mercy when the dogs attack you. I promise, I will watch them eat you alive."

Both girls' minds wandered back to the pyre, to Alex's broken body and bruised face. Surely, the monsters that had done that to Alex were capable of doing the same to them. That only meant one thing: that the escape had to work, or they would join Alex where he lay.

Chapter 12

Call the Doctor

Cain opened the door to a blast of frigid air. Awkwardly, he looked down at a 4' 8," ninety-pound Asian woman. He ushered Doctor Mauve Jewell into the kitchen and said, "Sorry to bring you out on a night like this, Doc, but I've a sick kid who needs your attention." He showed Doc Jewell into the bedroom where Ae Cha lay clawing her stomach and groaning. She had gotten vomit on herself and the smell was wafting through the air.

As Doc Jewell leaned on her cane and peered at Ae Cha, the girl pleaded, "It hurts so badly. Please stop the hurting,"

Doc Jewell took in her surroundings and said in a heavily accented voice, "You expect me to examine a child in this dishabille?" She grabbed a folded mat from her shabby medical bag, and returning to the kitchen, spread it over a dark stained table. She turned and directed Cain. "Put the girl on the table, so I can examine her. And, can you get me something sturdy to stand on, and more light?"

In no mood to suffer complaints, Cain protested, "Cut the crap, Doc. You're paid extremely well to treat these kids under any conditions. This isn't a five-star Wellness Center." Cain said acerbically while carrying a squirming Ae Cha over to the table. He set her down on the surface, not too gently. Then he positioned a stepstool that he removed from the pantry, on the floor before the table.

"You don't do a very good job of keeping kids healthy, from what I see in that funeral pyre deep in the woods." Cain recoiled; if she had seen that, who else might have come across it? Stepping onto the ladder, facing Ae Cha, Doc Jewel bristled, "How can the best of physicians cure these children after what's been done to them by human beasts."

Cain pivoted towards the door. "I'll get a camper's lantern from my van." He didn't worry about what happened to the kids, as much as he was paid to keep the kids and avoid authorities. He tried to ignore the collateral damage as just that, something that came with the territory. Once the kids were in his care, it wasn't like they were ever going home again.

Beneath sufficient light and with capable fingers, Doc Jewell examined the squealing girl. She gave her a sedative, stepped cautiously off the stepstool and wiped her hands with sanitizer from her bag. "Get her ready. I'm taking her with me for a few days. She's in no condition to be an escort. What is her name?"

"Ae Cha," Cain answered, his lips tight. He was going to be zero for three when Master next showed up, and there was only an acceptable explanation for one.

"Ae Cha needs antibiotics. She needs nourishment and good hygiene. If she doesn't get immediate care, her fate will be like the others." Her brow puckered. "And let me look at your ear. Foolish boy, why are you stretching your earlobe?"

"It's none of your business, Doc. But thanks for taking a look. It hurts like hell." He yanked the disc out of his other ear and tossed it on the table. "There, I'm done with that fad. Is this ear okay?"

Doc Jewell squinted her eyes, nodded and swabbed the swollen ear with an ointment. "It's abscessed. Hot pack it three times a day. It's infected so take these antibiotics until they're gone." She handed him a container of pills.

"What's wrong with Ae Cha?" Cain asked, giving a hand as Doc Jewel slipped Ae Cha's arms into a grimy yellow jacket. Ae Cha lay limp, like a rag doll, after taking the sedative.

"Accelerated hypertension, and I suspect inflammation of the stomach which can turn serious fast."

"Is it contagious?" Cain raised a hand to his forehead.

"Can be," Doc Jewel's eyes were unnervingly direct. "If you feel symptoms, call me immediately."

He considered a nasty reply and thought better of it. He said, "I'm not sure Master will go along with you removing Ae Cha from here, Doc."

"Cain, he may be your Master, but he's my equal! I had a discussion with him before I came here, and he is well aware that too many children have died from being in unsanitary conditions for too long a time." She repacked her medical bag and zipped it. "If he keeps piling diseased bodies in the woods and torching them, someone's bound to come across the carnage and draw attention to the authorities. Hikers and woodsmen aren't numbskulls."

"A clean-up crew comes in right after the cremation and removes all evidence," Cain snapped. His heart sped up a bit that the evidence was still there now.

"Evidence is all over the place, you numbskull," she waved her thin hand to dismiss the subject. "From now on when a child is very ill, they come with me," Doc Jewell said firmly. "My equal agrees with this recommendation. He assures me he is making arrangements for sanitary housing for these children. After all, they're providing a unique service, and customers expect a healthy child, not a diseased one." She looked inquiringly around the room. "Where are the others? I may as well check everyone while I'm here."

Cain answered with tension in his voice. "They're sleeping, best not to disturb them." He hoped it would work. Doc Jewell would contact Master with the truth faster than he could cover his tracks.

"Where's Amalia?" Doc Jewell looked puzzled.

Cain distractedly put his hand up to his sore ear and winced. His voice was guarded as he said, "She's in the woods looking for firewood to start a fire in the fireplace. We need to get the dampness out of here."

Doc Jewell said abruptly, "You're lying, Cain, but I don't care as long as it doesn't pertain to me. And if you *are* going to make a fire, be sure that chimney is unobstructed, or you'll have worse problems than being cold." She waved him and Ae Cha on. "Let's be off and remove your vile dogs and their filthy crates from my van. Nasty creatures. They yipped and drooled all the way here."

The tiny, wrinkled woman regarded him sidelong a moment with taunting eyes. "Strange, I've seen the loathing in Amalia's eyes when she looks at these beasts. Odd she's going to tolerate them being here now." She shook her head and shrugged her shoulders at the same time. "What's going on Cain?"

Cain brushed past her with Ae Cha to avoid the question.

Chapter 13

Interrogation

Police Captain Joe Dillon navigated the maze of corridors linking the cells at the chilly and bleak Plainfield, New York prison. The darkness in the halls and the chill in the air was reminiscent of every prison movie available.

As he passed through a series of security checkpoints, he was aware of a great deal of beeping and ringing from an assortment of electronic equipment. Video cameras were everywhere as he marched past shadowy, foul smelling chambers.

His guard escort led him into a small, sparse visitor's room and offered him a metal folding chair. Nothing could have prepared him as he looked upon the remnant of Will Inglis. Once a six-foot-five, two hundred seventy-five-pound man, Will's present state embodied what a lengthy incarceration can do. Pale and thin with swollen eyes, minus at least seventy-five pounds, the handcuffed man sitting in the cubicle behind the grill had his legs secured by a ball and chain attached to his chair.

Dillon anticipated the moment he would tell Lester how '*the Ace*' was doing. Not so cushy. It will make his day.

Dillon spoke first. "Hello, Will."

Inglis twiddled his thumbs.

"Straight to the point then," Dillon said. "I need to know what is going on at your farmhouse, or rather what went on at your farmhouse recently. Four local kids are missing, and we have good reason to believe they were being held at your farm for child sex-trafficking purposes. One girl is the daughter of a former associate of yours, Riley Wilkes." He stared at the smirk on Inglis' face. He wanted to wipe it off, and he was having a hard time keeping his cool. This was serious business. The inmates' casual demeanor was exasperating to the lawman. "Tell me what you know."

Inglis raised his eyebrows. "My sentence gets shorter if I become an informant?"

It bothered Dillon that Inglis' gaze was cool and direct, showing no sign of nervousness, even though he was a wreck of a man. "You know the system, Will, wash our hands, we'll wipe yours."

"This happened on your watch, Dillon. I should sue you and your department for negligence for not protecting my property while I'm in this hellhole. Whoever this sleazy bunch is, they physically broke in without my knowledge." Inglis' lips curled in disgust.

"Your part-time security guard is responsible for taking care of your farm, not the state or county." Dillon said briskly. "Tell me, is Cain deSantos involved in sex-trafficking?"

Will shook his head. "Cain's a boy scout, for cripes sake. He wouldn't tickle a frog. That's why I hired him."

"Cain's nowhere to be found. He is number one on our most wanted list. We learned he was on the job at your place for three months, and then about the time the kids disappeared, he vanished. He's missing from his Armory security job too. His employer is concerned and enlisted our help to find him."

Inglis wheeled back in his chair and slapped the ledge. "I spoke to Cain last week. He said everything's fine. And what about his cousin, Amalia? You find her, I guarantee you'll find him." He sneered. "Now Amalia's more apt to be involved in sex-trafficking than Cain."

Dillon looked puzzled. Here, indeed, was a lead. There's been no reference to Amalia. "Tell me what you know about her." Dillon was quiet for a time, willing Inglis to open up. He had hoped the silent treatment would cause an uncomfortable shift in the chain of authority between the men. Inglis was clearly in control, even from behind bars. He had mastered the art of few words.

Inglis made a sound of annoyance. "Dillon, you ask too many questions. Time for my nap. Guard!"

"What's the story on Cain and Amalia?" Dillon persisted.

A thick bodied guard appeared.

"We're not done here," Dillon waved him away.

Grunting, the guard dropped down in his chair, a breathing space away.

Will stretched his back and yawned. "The deSantos' have work visas allowing them to be in the US from Sweden. Amalia's a domestic... housekeeping, nanny, nurses aid." He winked. "A few things on the side. Man, she's a killer."

"What about Bud Phoenix? Can you give me background on him?"

Inglis replied instantly, "Harmless old drifter. He ran errands for me on the farm. Can't tell a dog from a cow. I let him pick around the place for tossed bottles. He cashes 'em in."

"We're grilling him now. We have a witness who saw him harassing the Wilkes girl at Storm Mountain Park before she went missing. And..." He let the sentence hang before continuing, "...he was seen speaking to a man resembling Cain deSantos." Dillon regarded Inglis levelly, satisfied there was a flicker of alarm in his eyes.

"No big deal," Will said matter-of-factly. "Bud and Cain know each other. They were chummy at the farm."

After draining a bottle of water, Dillon said, "Let me give you a quick overview. Last week, your farmhouse was headquarters for child sex-traffickers. A local resident spotted suspicious activity going on in your yard."

"Who? What business was it of theirs, eyeing my yard?" Will demanded. "I want to know who is snooping around my place." This little piece of information turned the table on who had the upper hand.

Dillon ignored Will and went on, "We sounded an alarm to one of our teams to go directly to your farm and rescue the kids. Of course, that didn't happen... the kids were taken somewhere else."

Will showed no glimmer of recognition on his face. Dillon was watching to be able to pounce.

"We realize there's a snitch in our group," Dillon continued. "We need to find the new location where the kids are and figure out who the snitch is."

Will replied angrily, "I know zip about it."

"If you're not involved, and I'll give you the benefit of the doubt, then the ringleader has to be someone you know well. Someone who could come and go in your farmhouse." He pitched forward in his chair to let Will mull over what he was about to say. "Who is almost as smart as you, that could pull this off?"

Inglis threw back his head and roared. "There's no one as capable as I am." He ticked two counts off his thick fingers and said in a deep angry voice. "First, I want to see my lawyer. Second, I need to make four phone calls."

Dillon stood up abruptly. "Call your lawyer and one other person, that's it. I'll be back at four this afternoon."

Will said belligerently, "If I get a good deal from the state, you'll have names. No one gets the best of Will Inglis. I was into dogfighting, not kid sex-trafficking. There's a difference."

You're still a dirt bag, Will. Dillon thought as he turned and went out.

Chapter 14

Big Bad Kitty

"The cat's name is Hopper." David announced, as he and Lester strolled into Mae Bolton's aromatic kitchen. Outside, on the wrap-around porch, Paddy and Patches slurped water out of deep ceramic bowls set out for them. They furiously shook dribbles off their chins, collapsed beside a rattan swing and lay down their heads, nodding off.

"How's the big guy?" Lester's tired eyes searched the occupied cat beds, set in a row, on the gleaming tile floor. When there was no sign of Hopper, Lester remarked, "Still around, I hope. David wants to see him."

Mae chuckled. "That darn cat's fit and sassy... he's a roamer... hasn't been around much the last two days." She was spinning fleece into thread using a distaff and spindle.

"Takes off, does he? That's a good sign he's fit," Lester said with a certain degree of amazement. "I thought he was a goner when I brought him here."

"He'll be back when he's hungry," Mae said assuredly. A clump of fleece was attached to the wooden distaff, which was supported in her left hand. The end of the thread was tied to the spindle and being rotated as she spun the thread through the fingers of her right hand. "Hopper and I get along just fine, as long as I don't try to corral him. Tell me, how did you find out his name? I've been calling him 'Big Bad Kitty.'" Saying his new name curled the sides of her mouth into a kind smile as she thought fondly of his sassy attitude.

"Long story, and I'll make it short." Lester leaned into the countertop, crossing his arms across his chest. "I was explaining to my nephew, Police Captain Joe Dillon... Joe's the head of the kidnapping task force..."

Mae nodded her head. "I know him and his family. Great guy and good looking too. Takes after his uncles."

Lester continued, "I told Joe how I found a wounded cat in the woods, and I brought him to you for patching-up. David was being interviewed by Joe, at the station, concerning his sister's disappearance. Well, David recognized my description of the cat and said it was a stray cat the neighborhood was feeding. He told how Caroline adopted it, despite her mother forbidding it. She named it Hopper."

"Cause sometimes he hops like a bunny," David spoke up.

"So, I've noticed," Mae's lips turned down. "And there's no sign of Caroline or the other children?" She looked questioningly at Lester.

Lester tried to hide how anxious he was from Mae and David, but Mae saw right through him. "Just a few bits and pieces here and there, but nothing to sink our teeth into."

Mae persisted, "I know David is staying with you, while his mom's recuperating at Joyful Haven, but please tell me there's hope of finding these children." Mae wasn't one to mince words. She knew that David had heard what was going on, and that sooner or later, he would figure out what was going on in the minds of the adults. In her mind, they shouldn't shield him from the truth. Until this ring was caught, the children of Grayridge, and surrounding areas, should be on guard.

Lester walked over to the round kitchen table covered by a floral tablecloth and cut two chocolate chip squares from a pan cooling on a rack. He kept one for himself and gave one to David. While he poured two glasses of goat's milk, he related to Mae the up-to-date happenings concerning the kidnappings.

"What evil there is in this world?" And before Mae could speak another word, a loud barking erupted in the front yard.

Lester, David, and Mae flew to the door and raced onto the porch.

A short, thick-set man of fifty, or thereabouts, was dragging a large green garbage bag behind him. "Here kitty, kitty." His thick fingers waggled in the air at Hopper.

Spitting and hissing, Hopper's back was straight up. A low growl erupted from his belly and continued as he backed further away from the man.

Mae flew down the steps and ran over to the man edging toward the cat. "Leave the cat be. He's been injured. If you lay hands on him, he'll scratch you or worse."

Bud Phoenix shifted the bag to his other hand and empty bottles spilled out. He bent down and grumbling, swiped them back into the bag. When he stood up, he snarled, "I was picking bottles off the side of the road. The cat passed right by me. I just wanted to pet it." He shrugged his shoulders.

"It's my sister's cat," David yelled. "Mrs. Bolton's taking care of it for her. Just leave it alone, mister."

Paddy and Patches scratched the dirt and barked.

"Glad I'm so mighty popular around here. Git these mutts away from me." Bud kicked air at the dogs.

Lester shouted above the frenetic barking and growling. "Paddy, Patches stay!"

The dogs whined and settled down. Hopper slinked over to Mae. She scratched his neck. He purred.

Bud looked at Lester with hard, probing eyes. He switched his dark gaze to Mae and then to David. Tossing the half full bag of bottles and cans over his shoulder, he huffed a cantankerous laugh and trudged down the road.

"I've seen him before," Lester watched the picker's back retreat in a northerly direction.

"He picks bottles in town." David frowned. "He's weird."

"Strange, Hopper's reaction to him was fierce." Lester rubbed his chin unrelenting. "Now it comes to me... my old brain ain't working as it should, "...that picker is on the list to be interrogated by Dillon... I believe his name is Bud Phoenix. And we better keep a close eye on Hopper. I think he can take care of himself, but just in case, we don't want anything to happen to him after all he's been through."

David stared fixedly at the bottle man lumbering down the road dragging a bag of bottles and cans behind him.

Chapter 15
Deals Delivered

"We have one good lead," Dillon announced hastily. He stood behind the desk in his office with his hands splayed on a stack of papers. On the other side of the desk, Lester and David sat rigid on battered folding chairs.

Having their attention, Dillon proceeded on. "The ticket agent at Storm Mountain State Park told our investigator that a young girl, resembling Caroline, stood in the promotion give-away line on the date she went missing. The girl walked away with a ticket for a gondola ride on Memorial Day weekend."

"I knew it!" David whooped, nearly upending a cup of paper clips with his flapping hands. "My sister went to the park to get a ticket for the gondola ride. She goes nuts for those rides."

Dillon raised his hand, indicating he had more to say. "The ticket agent threatened to call the cops on a man resembling Bud Phoenix, because he was harassing the girl. The ticket agent had words with the alleged Phoenix, threatening to call the cops if he didn't leave the girl alone, and he gave her a hard time before he moved on."

"I had a feeling that creep was involved somehow," Lester related the incident with Bud Phoenix at Mae Bolton's house and the bottle collector's interest in the stray cat.

"Do you think he was trying to get Hopper into the bag?" David raised his eyebrows.

Lester took a sharp intake of breath. "Not sure... but it appears that's what he was doing."

"Why?"

"Son, that remains a mystery, hopefully, to be solved one day." Lester turned back to Dillon. "How did the interview with Phoenix go?"

Dillon shook his head. "Couldn't get enough dirt out of him to put him away. Because he was the last to see Caroline Wilkes, he's a person of interest, and we're watching him closely. We hope he may eventually be the one to slip up and lead us to the kids and the perps."

Dillon's adrenaline was pumping. "Now back to what I was saying before the issue with the cat... in the same line where Caroline and Bud were standing, was Cain deSantos. According to the ticket agent, Cain and Bud made contact with each other. After they received their free ticket, the two men went separate ways." In a clipped voice, he added, "In the same time frame, Caroline disappeared."

"One of those guys took my sister?" David gasped.

"We're on it, Buddy." Dillon glanced at his watch. "David, I need to talk to Lester. It's official business. Sorry, but you can't be in on this." Time was of the essence with the emerging information, so he was rushing people along to get to the important part—searching.

David puffed out his cheeks and huffed. "What do you mean I can't be in on this meeting? It's *my* sister who's missing."

"Tell you what, David," Lester chimed in. "You best get over to Mae's and help her with chores, you know, feeding those cats, goats, and all her other animals? Check on Hopper for your sister. I'll pick you up later."

David's head snapped up. "Don't bother to pick me up, Lester. I'll walk. And, I don't need your help finding Caro! I'll find her myself." He stood up and hurtled through the door.

*****

"He'll get over it," Dillon's lips turned down. "Everyone's at the breaking point. Did you process what I told you this morning?"

"Do you mean to tell me Riley Wilkes would kidnap and prostitute his own daughter?" Lester raged. His bad knee stiffened, and he stretched his foot in front of him until the pressure eased.

Dillon dropped down in his chair, stretching his arms in front of him. "It doesn't appear Riley expected Caroline would be taken and used by the traffickers. But when it comes down to it, he'll save his own skin at the expense of his daughter. We have a tight lead that Wilkes is an agent in the kidnapping, prostitution, drug, pedophile, and pornography ring. We have everyone named except the person who is referred to as Master." He tapped a pen up and down. "In other words, we have the butcher, the baker, the candlestick maker, and the priest."

In a rare moment, Lester loaded his pipe and tamped it. "Let me guess where you got your information." He sucked on his pipe and released smoke in the air.

"Twice, I visited Will Inglis in jail. After he spoke to his lawyer, and he made a deal with the DA, he cooperated by giving us a list of names possibly affiliated with this group. He claims he isn't privy to the name of Master, and I tend to believe him. The order of who oversees the operation changes frequently."

"Inglis isn't getting a free pass out of jail, is he?" Lester shifted vigorously in his seat.

Dillon shook his head. "We need whatever input he can give us. This is one nasty affair, and a lot of local people are involved. We must be absolutely sure any information we get is correct before we go knocking on doors."

"Who are these scumbags?"

Dillon tapped a small pad in his pocket. "We're going to interview names on this list to determine whether they are guilty or innocent. We need to break them down, one by one, to get a lead to the location of these kids." He paused. "First on the list to be interviewed is Riley Wilkes."

Chapter 16
Daddy Dearest

The meeting was originally scheduled to be at Patterson's Auto Dealership, where Riley Wilkes worked in a cubicle which was in close proximity to several salesmen and women. However, realizing the conversation would be disconcerting, Riley insisted the meeting take place at Kevin's Bistro, two miles down the road from the office.

Kevin's Bistro was a popular tavern crowded with businessmen, truckers, and idlers. Riley was anxiously awaiting Dillon and Lester outside the restaurant. He tossed a lit cigarette onto the concrete sidewalk, stamped it, and waved them inside. "Let's be quick. I have a lot of catching up to do at the office."

Riley was a ruggedly handsome man, standing 6' 2." He looked tired, red-eyed, and his hands betrayed his nervousness as they shook slightly. Still, he drew glances from the ladies, dining out or waitressing, as he entered the popular restaurant.

They found a booth on the side wall and made their way through the noisy crowd to claim it.

A hefty, blond waitress appeared at the table. "Hi, the usual, Riley?"

Riley cleared his throat. "I'll have a ginger ale with lots of ice and a lemon, Misty."

Bemused, Misty nodded. "Gentlemen?" She asked Dillon and Lester.

"Coffee," said Dillon. "Cream and an artificial sweetener."

"Same beverage," said Lester. "Black."

After Misty shambled away, Riley made it known he was not pleased with Lester's presence. "I thought it was going to be you and me, Dillon."

Dillon explained. "Lester's part of the investigative team, Riley. I need backup for this conversation."

"If you need backup, do I need my lawyer? You alluded to confirming my statements about Caroline's disappearance." Riley's voice was guarded, and he pushed back in his seat. "Say, this smells like a dead rat. I gave you pertinent information at the house. Why haven't you found my daughter? You and the entire police force are worthless."

There was no tactful way, and Dillon took little time in choosing his words. "Due to an ongoing investigation led by the state police, Major Crime Unit, we have evidence you and others in this community have been selling your daughter, and other children, for sex to human traffickers."

Riley's lips curled in loathing as Dillon's words pulverized him. He stood up abruptly. "I'm not saying anything more until I see my lawyer."

Dillon said furiously. "Where are the kids, Riley? Caroline's your daughter, for god's sake. If you have any decency left, tell me." Dillon was an upright lawman all the way through, like the olden day movies portrayed, but in this moment, he wanted to knock the truth out of Riley Wilkes. What scumbag father could know what was happening to his child and act debonair with the authorities?

The fury in Riley's eyes caused Lester to flinch. Riley swung around nearly plowing into Misty carrying a tray of beverages. He elbowed through the crowd and left the bistro as if the devil chased him.

*****

Contemplating his coffee, Lester asked, "What's the object here, Dillon? You're close to finding the kids by pressing the likes of Bud Phoenix and Riley Wilkes. They're unraveling by degrees. I'm confused. Lay it on me."

"The detectives and troopers in the Major Crime Unit, I and my men, are lighting fires under the feet of these suspects," he nodded toward the exit where Riley went through moments before. "I expect at any moment one of them will cave in and give solid evidence leading us to the kids." Dillon wrapped his hands around his steaming mug. It was a long shot, and he hated waiting, but it was all they had at this time.

"I hate to dampen your optimism," Lester's gaze was cool and level. "What shape will these kids be in when you find them and what happens to 'em afterwards?"

Dillon peeled out several bills and left them on the table. He stood up, saying, "We have excellent organizations working together to benefit these kids. A *very* special lady is coordinating care, housing, and every resource imaginable for healing and recovery as we speak, but first we must find the kids."

"Do I know this wonder woman?"

"Mae Bolton."

They left the Bistro and inhaled the cool, clean outside air. "We have one more stop to make. Up to it? You're seeing a team in action."

"Where to, Dillon?"

"To the Happy Nails Salon to see a pedicurist. I need to talk to Hyun Ae and ask her why she sold her daughter, Ae Cha, to sex traffickers."

Chapter 17

Mother's Love

Lester peppered Dillon with questions the entire way to the Happy Nails Salon. Too caught up in his own thoughts to respond, Dillon shrugged Lester off, to his uncle's chagrin.

The parking lot at the salon was full. Paying no heed to *Do Not Park* signs, Dillon pulled the official car into a lined parking space, designated for customers, and turned the engine off. The two men left the vehicle and entered a small room in the rear of the building, having no need to disrupt clients and technicians in the occupational area.

They waited ten minutes before a petite oriental woman with bangs and straight gray/black hair, cut just below her ears, was ushered into the windowless room. An attendant closed the door as Hyun Ae's slanted eyes rolled suspiciously from Dillon to Lester.

"Who are you? Why are you here?" She asked in a barely audible, heavily accented voice.

Dillon showed his badge. "We are here about your daughter, Ae Cha."

A flicker of fear showed in Hyun Ae's guarded eyes. She said in a flash of anger. "Ae Cha... no more with me!"

"We know that, and now your child is our business. Ae Cha is being used for underage sex trafficking." Dillon flashed angrily back. "If you don't tell me who you sold her to, I'll turn you in to the head of the Crime Unit." He held up a pair of handcuffs, "In other words, Hyun Ae, I'm here to arrest you."

Hyun Ae glared at Dillon. Lester had seen wild animals in a trap with the same expression on their faces before, wild-eyed, and unsure how to escape in their desperation.

Dillon went on. "You are in this country illegally, and ICE will have no mercy on you when they become aware of this situation." He swiped his hand against a scarred wooden table, sending a stack of fresh white towels to the floor. No one paid attention. "It's your decision. You can tell me, right now, what you know and buy yourself time, or I can hear what you have to say in jail." Dillon wanted her to speak, but a part of him wanted her hidden in a cell.

"I was forced to sell Ae Cha." Hyun Ae complained. She reflexively rubbed her arm. The long sleeves and high-necked blouse she wore did not cover needle markings on her wrists, hands, and neck. "I have no money. What little I make here does not support her... us."

"You sold your daughter to support your drug habit. There was no concern at all for Ae Cha." Dillon found it hard to maintain his professional demeanor. Addicts were a problem. He had never fathomed dealing with an addict that sold her daughter. That was another level.

Hyun Ae said in broken English. "Need." She mimicked a needle being inserted.

Dillon snapped. "I want to find your daughter, and the other children, being sold for sex trafficking. We have the means to take care of them. We're not going to let up on this, understand?"

He pulled photos of thirty-four men and women out of a plastic folder and placed them face up on the table.

Lester picked up the towels, dropping them in a pile on a chair.

"Point to the man or woman who bought Ae Cha." Dillon said in a tone of voice that would not take no for an answer.

Hyun Ae waved her hands. "Na, na, you not understand. I brought Ae Cha to the parking lot here and left her by the Happy Nails Salon sign. I told Ae Cha someone would pick her up and take her for a ride. Money was left for me under a rock by the sign. I no see them. Don't make trouble for me. Go away." She closed her eyes tightly shut and began chanting.

"Hold out your hands. I'm going to cuff them." Dillon ordered.

Hyun Ae's eyes fluttered open.

The attendant poked her head in the doorway and said in an anxious voice, "Hyun Ae, your customer has been waiting for some time. He's threatening to leave if you don't service him now."

With a sigh, Hyun Ae tapped two photos from a group of local business owners and stated testily, "No want girl back. Under no circumstances do I want girl back." She darted out of the room.

"You gonna let her go?" Lester was shaking all over. He couldn't help himself.

Wearily, Dillon waved at Lester. "Don't worry, I'm going to notify ICE. They'll take care of Hyun Ae. We'll take care of her daughter. Come on, let's get out of here, before I start acting irrational."

Chapter 18

Hopper in the Lead

"David, what's wrong?" The tense expression on his face alarmed Mae.

"Nothin, 'cept…" David chewed his lip. "Oh, never mind, Lester told me to see you about chores and to check on Hopper, for my sister." He couldn't tell any adults that he was about to wage his own search. He knew they would lecture him and try to talk him out of it, or worse, order him not to go searching.

Mae nodded her head, surmising there had been a rift between David and Lester. She would mind her business, knowing Lester had only good intentions for the boy.

She smiled. "First things first. I'm going to make you a grilled egg, ham, and cheese sandwich with fried potatoes and onions. You can get ketchup out of the refrigerator." She walked to the cabinet and pulled a frying pan out of a drawer. Turning the stove on, she said, "You have that starved look on your face."

"I *am* hungry," David admitted, sliding the bottle of ketchup across the table, where it came to a miraculous stop at the edge. Before sinking into a chair, he helped himself to four peanut butter cookies from the cookie jar. "How's Hopper?" He asked with his mouth full.

Not wishing to comment on David's lack of manners, sliding the ketchup jar across the table and having a full mouth of cookies, Mae said, "He's been acting odd lately. For example, he takes off for a couple of days and comes back to wolf down bowls of food – my, that cat can eat. He also likes a good neck and ear scratch. Actually, he demands it... pampered cat."

While the potatoes and onions simmered in the pan, Mae sat down at the table and folded her hands in front of her. "What is odder still is the way Hopper tries to coax me to follow him. He acts like a dog begging for a walk. Let's see how he acts with you." Her eyes dropped to Hopper lying curled up in a cozy fleece bed with one striped paw covering an eye. "After his nap mind you, poor guy's exhausted from last night's high jinx."

*****

After eating a full, satisfactory meal and doing a round of chores, David went into the house, craving a glass of cold water.

When he went out on the porch, Hopper was sitting on the porch steps, cleaning the fur around his paw. Blinking once, his large, speckled gray eyes were directed at David.

"You trying to speak to me, cat? Your eyes are telling me something, I can feel it." He sat down next to Hopper and scratched his ears.

Warily at first, Hopper rubbed against David. Then he padded down the steps and went in the direction of the woods. At the edge of the woods, he turned around and stared at David, beckoning.

He wants me to follow him. David thought.

David called out to Mae through the open kitchen window. "I'm going to follow Hopper a ways. You're right. He wants to go for a walk. He thinks he's a dog." David was not going to let this opportunity slip through his fingers.

"Give me one minute," Mae hollered back. When she came onto the porch, she handed David a backpack. "There are treats and drinks in case you get thirsty or hungry. Also, treats for Hopper, Paddy, and Patches."

Two dogs burst through the door.

"Thanks Mrs. Bolton." David slid the backpack over his shoulders and ran toward Hopper. The dogs were already sniffing the trail.

Mae called after him, "Don't go too deep into the woods, just because Hopper does. Turn back after a while, he'll be alright. At least you can get an idea what he's up to. But please, bring the dogs back with you. I'm responsible for Paddy and Patches, and I don't want to deal with Lester if anything happens to them."

"Yes, Ma'am." David breezed down the worn grassy path and went into the shadowy woods. David hoped that Hopper knew the way to Caroline. She sure loved that cat.

Chapter 19

A Cova

"I think we're going in the right direction," Caroline, breathing heavily, said to Lily Moon.

Chilled to the bone in the first light of day, the girls were crossing a flat, slippery expanse of mountain rock. Exhaustion levels had peaked, yet they continued on to make it to safety.

"Where are we?" Lily Moon, on the edge of coming unraveled, asked. Adrenalin and fear coursed through her bloodstream as she clung to the rocky ledge. Lightheaded and dizzy, she averted her eyes from the overpowering, steep panorama stretched out below her. When her eyes fixed on the view, she stumbled and slammed her hands and knees into crushed stone, crying out in pain.

"I wish your cat was still with us," she gasped. "He seemed to know where he was going," Lily Moon rolled over and pulled herself back up to standing position.

"At least I know Hopper's okay. He'll find us again." Caroline said assertively.

Elsewhere, a thunderous barking exploded.

Caroline whipped her head up. "C'mon, Lily Moon! Cain and Amalia are here with their dogs. We've got to hide." The girls pounded down the steep rock as fast as their feet could go. Sheer willpower pushed them into thick brush, where brambles and briers tore at their exposed skin.

Out of breath, they came upon a creek splashing through its bed and followed it a way before stopping. Satisfied they had put distance between them and the dogs, Caroline cupped her filthy hands, filling them with clear water, and drank. The cool water quenched her dry throat. She hadn't realized how thirsty she was until she was able to drink.

Lily Moon gulped the bracing water and sighed as it trickled down her throat.

With numb legs and feet, they splashed upstream in the frigid waters, hoping to throw the dogs off their scent.

Suddenly, as a heart stopping racket drew nearer to them, Caroline pointed to a large opening in a massive rock. "Look, Lily Moon."

"A cova." Lily Moon whispered reverently, and she made the sign of the cross.

*****

Inside the cove, the air was musty and cold. As their eyes adjusted to the dusky interior, Caroline and Lily Moon were amazed to see a bright light shimmering where the rock surface slanted downwards into an immense cavern. Beyond, shooting stars glittered in a spectacular array.

Lily Moon sprinted to the illumination. She dropped to her knees, blessed herself, and raised her eyes to the exposition.

Caroline stared into the brightness and saw nothing. She rubbed her eyes to purge the extreme glare, causing them to fill with blinding tears.

"Lily Moon, what do you see?" She blinked.

Lily Moon's lips parted and moved slightly, "Hail Mary, full of grace ..."

*****

Half a mile away, two growling pit bulls tore across the mountain ledge. Following in close pursuit were Cain and Amalia. Their frantic voices were lost on each other amid the frenzied howling of fierce, angry dogs. One dog stopped abruptly, sniffing and licking a spot on the rock. Their muscles flexed as they pulled on their leashes, pulling their leads against Amalia and Cain.

"Hannibal's caught the scent," Cain yelled as the dog howled and bared his fangs.

Amalia huffed belligerently, "Must these brutes be so noisy? They've announced our presence for sure."

Cain exclaimed. "Look! There's blood on the rock. One of the girls must have cut herself."

Amalia's eyes were slanted as she sneered. "We're closing in. Show us the way, brutes."

Chapter 20
Closing In

Trailing Paddy, Patches, and Hopper up the steep mountain slope was no easy task. It annoyed David having to call the dogs often, as they would veer off on new trails and take their time returning to the original one. Mrs. Bolton's words burned in his mind, *"Bring the dogs back, or I will have to deal with Lester."* He knew Mrs. Bolton feared Lester's distress if anything happened to Paddy or Patches. Now the responsibility was on his shoulders, and he felt a heavy burden wash over him.

Upwards, they clambered until the air became thin. He whistled to the animals to halt. The dogs came promptly to him. Hopper's lackadaisical manner was irritating. When David shook the treat bag, the cat hopped over to him readily.

After the treat break, consisting of milk bones and nuggets for the dogs, party mix for Hopper, and cold milk, cookies, and an apple for David, they ventured down a dirt road overgrown with bushes and vegetation. Overhead branches formed a leafy tunnel through which David, the dogs, and Hopper passed. At the path's end, a crude hunting lodge appeared.

Torn between checking out the lodge or following Hopper down the trail, David chose to search the lodge. It was getting late, and he owed it to Mrs. Bolton to get the dogs back before dark. She had assured him Hopper would return home in his own good time.

"Take care, stubborn ol' cat." He watched Hopper trot off and disappear into the woods.

*****

David made his way into the creaky, groaning camp, and the first room he entered was the kitchen. Even though the area was bare, there was evidence of recent occupancy. The air smelled of mold, rust, antiseptic, and spoiled food.

Were you here, Caro, with the other kids?

There was a sound behind him. The hairs on his arms stood on end. He almost screamed, then with great relief, Paddy and Patches whizzed past him, sniffing at every nook and cranny.

"Whew, you guys, I'm losing it!" He gasped. He had felt brave until encountering this remote lodge.

In the hallway, he mounted the narrow, steep stairs,

turning right at the top landing. He continued to climb the two additional steps to a corridor. He checked out all the bedrooms. There was nothing except ragged curtains hanging from undersized high, grimy windows ushering in insignificant light.

Descending the stairs, he went into a room off the kitchen. Three blankets were tossed to the sides of old mattresses. Patches was sniffing and scratching at something.

David went over and peered down. "Here boy, let me see that." Patches relinquished a leather headband with yellow flowers painted on it. David's cheeks were flushed as he let out a whoop. "Caro's dorky headband! Good boy, Patches! We've got to get Lester and Dillon up here, pronto."

With the two dogs in tow, David raced down the mountain at Olympic speed. At times, he tumbled head over heels, cementing blood and gravel on the palms of his hands and knees.

At the Bolton farmhouse, David skidded into the kitchen, catching himself before he slammed into the kitchen table. He leaned over and grasped the table's edge. Many emotions raced through him as he relaxed, safe at last in familiar territory.

Mae dropped her knitting in a basket, rose up from her glider chair, and exclaimed, "Oh my, what's happened? Not the animals!" Then she saw Paddy and Patches empty their water bowls on the porch.

David showed her his bloody hands and knees.

Mae clapped her hands to her face.

"I've got to find Dillon and Lester right away. I know where Caro is!" He struggled to catch his breath.

Mae ran a washcloth under warm tap water, squeezed it, and handed it to David. "Clean those cuts." And with shaking hands, she tapped in the number of Lester's cell phone.

Chapter 21

Desperation

"Why are the dogs acting loopy?" Amalia shouted to Cain, a bandage covering his sore misshapen ear as he walked fast a few yards ahead of her.

After Hannibal and Caesar repeatedly failed to enter the woods, they lay down, yawned, and dropped their massive heads on their paws.

"Where's the goddamn whip?" Amalia snapped at Cain. He frantically clapped his hands and yelled, "Scent! Hannibal, Caesar, scent!" The dogs didn't bother to look up at their master.

Amalia slapped her hands on her hips, "What do you make of this, Cain? These brutes have become docile. Damn, we don't need this hassle." Her dislike of the beasts rushed back in full force.

Cain blew out a perplexed sigh. "If I didn't know better, it appears we've encountered a forcefield."

The blood rushed hot into Amalia's face. "Do something! We've got to find the girls and bring them back to the camp." She stared at her watch, panicking at the time.

"Master's coming tonight. He wants to take Caroline with him."

Cain looked out at the far-reaching panorama and gauged the distance below their present location. "Our only chance is for me to go down the mountain and cut into the woods beyond the forcefield." He hesitated. "One catch, you'll have to stay with the dogs. They would be a nuisance for what I have to do."

Amalia looked sideways at the two massive animals. She shook her head. "I don't want to be alone with them."

"You must. They would only get in my way trying to maneuver past this forcefield." The terrain was tricky, and if the dogs were stubborn, or decided to go their own way, they could have him toppling down the mountain.

"Then hurry!" Amalia wrung her hands. "We'll keep in touch with cell phones."

"Don't panic if we don't get reception. We're in the mountains." Giving a half-hearted wave, Cain began his descent down the wide area of steep mountain.

*****

Caroline leaned her back against the damp chill of the cavern wall. Without realizing what she was doing, she scratched at the wall, and dried honeybees fell into her hands. She was so hungry she ate one, deciding they did not taste too bad and scratched for more to eat.

Meanwhile, Hopper slipped inside the cave. He stared into a bright light and witnessed a beautiful lady speaking softly to Caroline's friend.

The rapture went on for some time. Then the light dimmed and faded.

Lily Moon sat very still for several minutes. When she was able to move, she stood up and wandered over to Caroline, who was squatting on the dank, wet floor, petting Hopper. She beamed, "When we get back to the village, there are things we have to do."

"What things?" Caroline asked, munching on the dried bees.

Lily Moon stared through the cove's entrance to the brightness outside. Her revelation cut deep into the woods. "We must pray the rosary every day, say Hail Mary's often, and go to mass on Sundays and holy days."

"That's a Catholic thing, isn't it? I'm not Catholic." Caroline frowned. "Actually, I don't belong to any religion. My mom and dad never took me to a church." She squeezed Hopper tighter than she should have. He squirmed out of her reach and licked the fur on his back.

"I promised the Blessed Mother we would do those things for her." Lily Moon said curtly.

Caroline gazed at the area in the cove where the Blessed Mother appeared. She could not explain the sudden spiritual feeling she experienced, and she answered, "Lily Moon, teach me how to pray like you do."

Lily Moon heaved a sigh. "I will, Caroline, as soon as we figure out how to get out of here and back to safety." She sighed. "Then the first thing we must do is to get help for Ae Cha."

Caroline pulled a handful of dead bees out of her pocket. "Here, eat these. I got them out of the cave wall. They take hunger pains away."

"I'm so hungry, I'll eat anything." Lily Moon closed her eyes and popped them into her mouth, grimacing. "Yuck ..." She continued to munch on them, even though her tastes were contrary to eating bugs.

*****

Cain entered the woods three miles down the mountain from where Amalia and the attack dogs waited. He walked an approximate mile in, turned abruptly, and began his ascent. The trail was so steep and embedded with wild patches of sticker bushes, it was a struggle to climb back up the mountain. Sweating profusely, and beyond thirst, he dropped down on the ground in a clearing to catch a breath.

He took notice of the splashing of a mountain brook and crawling to the running stream, he gulped the water down.

With the brook dashing by him, and in the innate stillness, he sensed he had found his prey.

"Caroline, Lily Moon!" He cupped his hands and shouted. "I'm coming after you."

Caroline chewed on her knuckles. She had hoped to hear a different voice calling their names, but this was undoubtedly Cain calling.

Hopper squeezed his eyes tight and growled.

"Hail Mary, full of grace …," Lily Moon entreated.

Chapter 22

The Heat is On

Standing in the middle of Mae Bolton's sunny kitchen, with leafy shadows undulating on the walls from the majestic maple trees in her backyard, Dillon squeezed David's shoulder. "Good detecting, David. One day, you'll make a superior lawman." He scratched the fine growth of beard on his chin. "I can't take you with us. There may be gunfire and a possible nasty exchange with scoundrels. You'll have to stay with Mae."

"I'm goin' to that cabin to search for my sister." David yelled. "You ain't stopping me agin." David felt jilted; he was the one who had found the cabin, and he'd already been inside once. There was no reason, in his mind, that he should be left behind.

Feeling knots tightening in his stomach, Lester piped up. "David can wait in the truck with me. We'll park on the road just below the cabin. I can't go in until it's all clear either, but I want to be close by. I'll be responsible for the boy. Sign a form, if need be."

Dillon pressed his lips together. "I may be taken down for this, you two. Remember when the time comes, I don't know anything about it. Let's go."

*****

After Dillon and his officers searched the deserted cabin, once owned by a Grayridge couple now deceased, and finding evidence of recent occupancy by truants, but no sign of Caroline or the other children, he blew a shrill whistle.

The moment Lester and David heard the all clear signal, they drove to the cabin.

Standing motionless outside the cabin, ears straining to hear any revealing sound that Caroline and the other captives were close by, Dillon and Lester listened to David's account of how Hopper had veered to the left of the house and continued down a narrow trail when he decided to search the cabin and found his sister's headband.

"I thought nothing of it at the time, figuring ol' Hop was just doing his roaming while the dogs and I went through the house." His eyes widened a little. "In his catty way, Hopper seemed to know exactly where he was going. I wonder… Paddy, Patches, here girls." David led Paddy and

Patches to where Hopper was last seen. Everyone stared at the dogs as they sniffed the ground and bolted forward.

The team charged two miles down the tight trail, which opened onto a large region of rocky mountain terrain. Ferocious barking erupted close by, and a tall, thick-bodied blond woman stared, with complete incomprehension, as two dogs and twelve lawmen marched toward her.

Amalia turned and ran screaming Cain's name echoing down the rocky ledge. Dillon raced after her, in good form, and tackled her to the stony ground. He avoided her kicks and was not quick enough to dodge a fist to his face, bloodying it. He tightened his grip on her while waiting for assistance.

Seizing control, Dillon roughly swung Amalia around and, with the assist of an agent, handcuffed her.

Nearby, the SWAT team fended off a major dog fight by tranquilizing Hannibal and Caesar, securing them in nets and chains. Lester stayed in command of Paddy and Patches, who remained by his side the whole time.

When the clash was over, and Dillon had secured Amalia to the helpful agent, David demanded, "Where's my sister?"

Amalia spat on the ground and before a word could be spoken, a shout came from nearby in the woods, "Get off me! Get this creature off my back. Amalia, help!" Cain shrieked. David's attention snapped to the new voice that was ringing clear from deeper in the woods.

Screams of acute agony were followed by a spine-tingling "pssst," as if a mountain lion was having his way with a defenseless prey.

"Something's attacking Cain. You must help my cousin!" Amalia pleaded, waving her shackled hands before her.

Amalia was held back firmly by the agent as Lester, Dillon, David, the lawmen, and two dogs leading, bounded in the direction of the ear-piercing shrieks. Scrambling through sharp, piercing brambles, a little distance into the woods, they found Cain struggling with Hopper, who was busy ripping flesh off his back.

David removed Hopper from Cain's bloodied back, and while an AMT agent applied first aid to Cain's wounds, Dillon read him his rights and handcuffed him. David held the cat and watched intently, until Hopper was satisfied that Cain was no longer a threat and jumped to the ground.

Lester, David, Paddy, and Patches followed Hopper inside the cove. There was a movement they caught at the corner of their vision, and they turned to see two bedraggled, cowering little girls.

"It's okay," Lester said gently. "You are safe."

The girls did not budge from where they huddled.

"Caroline?" David shouted.

Caroline burst into tears.

Tossing all self-conscious feelings aside, David ran to his sister, nearly tripping over Hopper, and swept her in his arms. He hugged her until she could not breathe.

Her eyes glazed over; she turned pasty white and fainted.

With Caroline clasped limply in his arms, David held her worn-out body until the EMTs attended her. Gently, and with tears streaming down his face, he hugged and kissed Caro. He resolved to never let her out of his sight again.

Chapter 23

Joyful Haven

It has been three weeks since Caroline Wilkes, Lily Moon, Ae Cha, and several other children were rescued from their captors.

The November day was brisk as Lester drove his truck east on Koles Highway. Further along, he shot off the ramp and turned left onto County Road 4. The afternoon sun shone cold, in a cloudless blue sky, over well-tended farmland. As he turned into Henry, a covered bridge crossing Platoon Creek, allowing entrance to a long, gravel driveway, he yodeled.

The truck approached the semi-circle at the end of the drive. In the center of the grassy divide rose a flagpole. The red, white, and blue flag snapped proudly in the wind. Mostly hidden, behind a huge sugar maple tree, stood a century-old farmhouse donated and renovated, with love and well-wishes, to Joyful Haven, a home for victims of human trafficking and modern-day slavery. These victims include youth, men, women, and children seeking refuge from abuse, neglect, abandonment, homelessness, and other complex circumstances.

Lester drove by a group of people gathered in a sunny area of an old-fashioned wrap-around porch. Men and women wearing fleece jackets and knit hats were drinking hot chocolate and munching cider donuts.

He continued around another semi-circle and parked the truck in the parking lot on the side of the house. As he left the truck and walked toward the porch, his eye caught the replica of an owl perched on the cupola on the pitched red shingled roof. Legends affirm owls symbolize luck, wisdom, and protection from suffering. Lester reflected: *These people have suffered enough in their lifetime. It's good to have an owl for a talisman in their temporary haven.*

A group of children nearly clipped him in their race to see who was first to get to play hide-and-seek behind an ancient maple tree. He grabbed onto one little guy, who was about to trip and fall to the ground, stopping him from the race. He plunked him firmly on his feet. The tyke tore off without uttering a word.

Lester approached the porch steps and said, "Hi everyone." The residents raised their mugs in salute, as he knocked on the broad front door.

An attendant opened the door, and Lester dropped his hands to his sides. "I'd like to see Mrs. Wilkes and Caroline. If you think it's too soon to speak to them, please say so."

Before the attendant could reply, Mae Bolton called out from the left side of the house, "Come in, Lester. Bridget will take you to the sunroom where the guests and residents are gathered." There was a sound of dishes clattering. "I'm in the kitchen making tea. I'll join you shortly."

"Hi Mae," Lester called down the narrow hallway leading to the kitchen. "I'll not stay long. I'll be leaving for the courthouse and Dillon's press release at 2:00."

"Perfect. Some of us are going in the van to represent Joyful Haven." Mae replied.

He followed a petite, dark-haired woman down a hallway made bright with wallpaper imprinted with multi-colored peonies. Bridget Mulligan said, "Mae is such a good person, Mr. Cranshaw. She's been with our coalition since its inception." They turned a corner and went deeper into the house. "It's because of Mae that Mrs. Wilkes is progressing satisfactorily. We didn't have much hope for her when she first came to Joyful Haven. She was demoralized by that brute of a husband, who was a member of a local and national sex trafficking group who abuse children, including his own daughter." She huffed and then brightened, "but, now that Mrs. Wilkes has her two children with her… under supervision at the Haven of course …"

"Yes, truly a miracle," Lester conceded.

"And to think the Blessed Mother appeared to Lily Moon in the cove…" Bridget shifted her eyes toward Lester. Her voice inflected a question, *is this true or did the girls make it up?*

Sensing her uncertainty, Lester sighed, "I know it's hard to believe, Bridget, but Lily Moon and Caroline are truly convincing when they describe the apparition of the Blessed Mother inside the cove. She appeared physically to Lily Moon, and Caroline backs it up by the ambiance she witnessed between Lily Moon and this vision." He paused and then continued. "A qualified team of church leaders, directed by the Pope in Rome, are investigating the apparition, and in time, they will make a decision whether it is authentic or not. Meanwhile, Lily Moon is unshakeable in her belief. She and Caroline say the rosary every day, and they plan to go to mass on Sundays and holy days." He removed his cap and scratched his head. "I find all of this incredible, Bridget, from the child trafficking, the kidnapping, the darn cat's role in this debacle, and the apparition of the Blessed Mother." He shook his head slowly; it had been a lot to process.

They stopped before a glass paneled door. Through the glass, Lester gazed into a room with chintz-covered sofas and chairs, a fieldstone fireplace and a long, trestle table flanked by ladder back chairs.

A frail Cheryl Wilkes sat in a chair by the lit fireplace half smiling at Caroline, Lily Moon, and Ae Cha. The latter was recuperating from a viral stomach illness. The fragile looking child appeared peaked and gray. They, and a group of boys and girls of varied ages and nationalities, were busily making beaded friendship bracelets.

A cluster of other children sat off to one side of the long table, quietly observing the others. From the look of suffering and distress on their young faces, it would be a while before they participated in any activity.

With a pain deep in his heart, Lester turned his gaze from those children and smiled as he spotted Hopper curled up, sleeping in a fleece-lined basket at Cheryl's feet. His fur appeared to have been brushed to a glistening coat, having burrs and debris removed. He wore a new red Seresto collar.

There was a fluttering at his back. "Coming behind you," Mae announced cheerily. "Lester, be a good man and open the door for me."

"I'll do better than that," He took the tray from her and pressed his back against the door, allowing the ladies to enter. He carried the tray into the room and set it on the table, away from the materials the kids were crafting with.

Tea, juices, and brownies were served while everyone visited. Lester made it a point to sit beside Cheryl.

"I want to thank you, Mr. Cranshaw, for helping find Caroline and being there for my David." She dabbed at her eyes with a linen hankie. Lester noticed it was Mae's handiwork on the handkerchief by the multi-colored crocheted edging.

"Commendations go to many people, Mrs. Wilkes," Lester said. "And please, call me Lester."

"Yes... Lester, I agree, but my allegiance goes directly to you and Officer Dillon. David thinks you and Officer Dillon are the greatest two people on earth. He wants to go into law enforcement because of Officer Dillon."

"How is David doing?" Lester asked.

Cheryl fixed her eyes on Lester's and said, "He has grown into a young man since this torrid affair. Unfairly, his childhood's gone." She fidgeted with a wooden button on her sweater. "Since he's living in the dorm, here at Joyful Haven, and working full time on this farm, we see each other often. He runs in from chores and says, 'Hi, ma.'" Cheryl smiled self-deprecatingly and added, "I don't deserve that. I have not been a good mother."

Lester raised his hand and was about to speak, however, Cheryl was intent on what she was saying and continued, "But I love and appreciate every minute with my children. In time, and with Mae's help... thank God for that woman... we'll be together as a family, just the three of us, out on our own. Thanks to the staff and time spent here at Joyful Haven, we'll be ready to take on the world again." She heaved a grateful sigh.

Bridget, shifting in her seat next to Lester, turned to address him, "I have a request for you from the staff at Joyful Haven."

Lester scrunched up his face and mimicked being attacked by a wild animal.

Caroline, Ae Cha, and Lily Moon giggled.

"And the answer is no, ladies." Lester said in a comical voice.

"Listen to the request, Lester." Mae chimed in. She was removing empty paper cups and plates from a side table and collecting them on a tray. "It might do you and I a good turn."

Bridget pushed on, "Since David is living and working here, Mae tells us you are minus a farmhand." She paused before commenting further. She had caught Lester's attention. He looked at her promptly. "There's a young man about to graduate from Joyful Haven's work program. Louis Mendezo is twenty-years-old and will need a place to live and a job to go to. He is trustworthy and ambitious, aspiring to pay it forward, since he escaped from a sex-trafficking cartel and has gained his life back at Joyful Haven. He plans to volunteer in his free time in one of our programs."

Mae leaned forward and said, "Louis is a wonderful young man, Lester. I expect he can live in the trailer on your property and do both of our farm chores. If we each pay him a fair salary, he should manage to live on that very well."

Lester watched Hopper climb out of his basket and pad to the treats in his antique, gold-edged Nippon bowl. He addressed Mae, "Sounds like the jury on Louis is in. I trust you will make the arrangements, Mae, and I look forward to meeting this young man, but not at this time." He looked at his watch. "I have to be at the press conference, at 2:00, with Dillon." He stood up, clapped his hat on his head, tossed a friendly wave, and exited the sun-filled room.

Chapter 24

Darkness Comes to Light

It was 1:45 in the afternoon when Lester parked his truck two blocks from the courthouse. He shambled down the crumbling sidewalk, on the once trendy tree-lined street. Not since the 1950's had the low-end, neglected houses seen better days. He detoured through a scruffy backyard, aiming to avoid the press corps, armed and ready for an explosion of news. As he was about to enter a side door of the quaint gray stone Municipal building, a reporter shouted his name. Lester zipped through the door and slammed it shut, avoiding the press like the plague.

Inside, reporters and cameramen milled about making final adjustments to their equipment. The spectator section was filled with 70% of angry town residents. 10% of Grayridge residents were either ill or incapacitated and would be there if their afflictions would allow. The final 20% were being processed for heinous crimes.

The seats in the historic building were elevated. Lester grabbed one in the back, where he surveyed the packed room. The anger in the room was so palpable it was noticeably in the air.

He spotted Mae Bolton, Margot Kelley, director of Joyful Haven, several Joyful Haven associates, and David and Caroline Wilkes seated, in the middle of the crowd, ten rows away from the podium. *Was that a cat carrier positioned at Caroline's feet?*

There was a buzz from a microphone. He snapped his attention back to Dillon, standing at the podium, flanked by a prestigious group of lawmen, who shared their time and expertise in the investigation, plus four police canines. Lester beamed at Dillon, who was about to make his opening statements.

Dillon waited for the press frenzy to settle down, and then he said, "Let me begin by announcing that an elaborate undercover operation revolving around money, politics, and child sex-trafficking shook our town of Grayridge to its very core. I can tell you, now, that every child we searched for has been found and is in a safe place." His hands gripped the back of the podium, "except for one. Sadly, four-year-old Alex Clarke's remains were discovered with approximately thirty-two children's corpses piled in a burial pyre, like debris, ready to be torched."

There was a gasp from the crowd and a moan from a woman standing on the side of the room wrapped in her husband's arms. "My condolences, Mr. and Mrs. Clarke,"

Dillon's voice shook as he spoke their names. He turned back to the crowd frozen in their seats, faces appalled.

After pausing to give the public time to recover, he continued, "Most of the perpetrators are citizens we trusted, and are committed to high offices, in our community. They covered up their atrocities by blatantly using their civic duties to attain power to buy drugs, pornography, while sex-trafficking our children."

A deep, angry voice erupted, "Let us have at these sons and daughters of Satan." A man in a white t-shirt with the script *Big Bruce* printed across his chest raised huge fists.

"Hear, hear," roared the crowd.

Dillon called for order, and it was several minutes before he could continue, "I understand your feelings, but you can't take the law in your own hands." He clenched the microphone, "There is one person in this group who was not what he appeared to be in our community. You know Shane Miller, as owner of Miller's Shoe Emporium. For the last two years, he earned the trust of these men and women by seeming to join in their escapades. Realistically, he was infiltrating their ranks and wooing the town's politicians and business owners over wine and tapas. It turns out Shane Miller is an undercover ICE agent. I will introduce you to him momentarily in his proper persona."

Dillon took a sip of bottled water and went on, "I need to address the alleged apparition of the Blessed Mother at the cove. I see many skeptical faces in this crowd, as you can see a similar expression on mine. In due respect to Lily Moon and Caroline Wilkes, there is strong evidence the Blessed Mother did appear to Lily Moon, and Caroline witnessed the sacred moment of the apparition. They have been questioned thoroughly and have been firm in their belief it is Our Lady who appeared on that memorable day. This matter is now in the hands of a religious group associated with the Pope and the Vatican hierarchies in Rome. They will determine the truth and make a judgment.

"Meanwhile, Grayridge will not be inundated with pilgrims visiting the cove. Thankfully, we have hotels and tourist locations to handle these visitors in our neighboring tri-cities: Richmond, Madison, and Gage City. A chapel is being erected at the cove, by members of local Catholic Churches, in honor of the Blessed Mother. A planning board is studying the effects on cost and traffic. There will be no tax burden on Grayridge; actually, the outcome should work in our favor.

"In conclusion, we have proved, beyond a reasonable doubt, thanks to Agent Miller, his team, my team, my Uncle, Lester Cranshaw, young David Wilkes, and a stray cat who now belongs to Caroline Wilkes, named Hopper, the following people are pedophiles, aided pedophiles, and were involved in sex-trafficking innocent children for their own pleasure. There is a great number of people who, by their inaction, are as guilty as the men and women who performed the heinous acts on these children.

"I am sorry to say, I trusted several of these men and women explicitly and considered them loyal friends." He stared intently at the spectators. "If you are uncomfortable hearing the names and titles of those once considered trustworthy in the Grayridge community, I suggest you leave now." His sharp eyes took in the entire crowd. "I guarantee some of these people will be your family members, neighbors, and friends. This day is apt to haunt you forever."

The spectators spoke in hushed voices. Several got up and left the room. Their empty seats were filled by others who were standing on the sidelines.

"I now direct you to Agent Miller."

Dillon moved off to one side as Agent Shane Miller stepped up to the podium. He had black hair peppered with gray, and he stood lean and lanky at 5' 9." He slid eyeglasses to the top of his cropped head and looked down at the papers he held in his hand. In a hard-hitting voice, filled with confidence, he addressed the crowd. "These people whose names you are about to hear, in no special order, are being processed at the jail as this press conference is in progress:

"Mayor Priscilla Kemp,

"Grayridge Town Board Member Alexander Clark,

"Grayridge Highway Superintendent Henry Franks,

"Polly Whitman, owner of Whitman's Restaurant,

"Reverend James Tully of Blessed Sacrament Church,

"Robert Toohey, Senior, Lawyer, Toohey and Co.,

"Robert Toohey, Junior, Lawyer, Toohey and Co.,

"Anthony Brand, Second Grade Teacher at Cormier Elementary,

"Connie Woo, Sixth Grade Teacher at Cormier Elementary,

"Lucinda Bates, Seventh Grade Teacher at Cormier Middle School,

"Officer James Levensworth, Grayridge Police Department,

"Abigail Meyer, housewife and Yoga Instructor,

"Marvin Patterson, owner, Patterson's Auto Dealership,

"Riley Wilkes, father of Caroline and David Wilkes, car dealer salesman, Patterson's Auto Dealership,

"Hyun Ae, Ae Cha's mother and manicurist at Happy Nails Salon,

"Huan Pasos, True Value Hardware owner,

"Sam Casey, owner, Grayridge Custom Meat & Smokehouse,

"Chelsea Noonan, owner, Hand knitting, Weaving, Spinning Supplies,

"Amalia and Cain deSantos, cousins, kidnappers, aided and abetted sex-traffickers,

"Bud Phoenix, kidnapper, aided and abetted sex-traffickers,

"There are many others who are about to be arrested, folks." Agent Miller rubbed his chin. "I would say 40 percent of Grayridge residents are involved, as are an equal number of outsiders. You have a good deal of cleansing to do in this community. I have worked in numerous places in America. Sad to say, this is the norm today. Like Inspector Dillon told you, it will never happen again under his watch. In Grayridge, it is the beginning of the end of child sex-trafficking. Keep your eyes open and your children close."

While a modicum of clapping occurred, Agent Miller turned from the podium and shook hands with Inspector Dillon and the others. He tapped the head of each service dog who raised a paw and shook his hand.

Standing on the podium, holding Hopper in her arms, Caroline beamed as Agent Miller tapped Hopper's head and shook his paw.

Agent Miller announced, "In August of this year, this hero cat will receive the Buddy Medal of Honor, presented to him by the newly elected mayor of Grayridge. God bless!"

Exiting the chamber, he acknowledged the teary crowd with a thumbs-up.

Chapter 25
Identities Revealed

"*Master* is three men, not one," Dillon explained with a solemn expression on his face to untainted lawmen, councilmen, religious leaders, and members of select Grayridge organizations. As an independent advisor, Lester Cranshaw sat in between Mae Bolton and Margot Kelley, representing Joyful Haven. The assembly sat at a long table, in a vast area, in the Municipal Town building. Bottles of water were set before each person.

Dillon counseled, "Thanks to the fine detecting of Agent Miller, this concept, which stymied us during the entire investigation, has been solved. Agent Miller broke down *Master* into three parts: a priest, an auto dealer owner, and a True Value Hardware owner. These three men managed to keep this top secret even from their kidnappers and all the others they employed to do their foul work. For instance, cousins Cain and Amalia deSantos met with the same person personified as *Master* every time they came together. That person was Huan Pasos. Occasionally, they would see Pasos, Father Tulley, and Marvin Patterson together, believing they were going about their activities separately, when indeed the trio were the persona *Master*. There was one person who knew of the set-up; Dr. Mauve Jewell was aware of the three persons as one, and she, too, has been arrested as an accomplice.

"It was protocol to have a child delivered to Pasos. In turn, he would pass a boy or girl on to a client in the network who paid for the child's services. When the transaction ended, Pasos, or one of the other men acting as *Master,* would deliver the child to the deSantos' for care and supervision.

"The work on these crimes is completed. Now, it is up to you, my fellow Grayridge neighbors and associates, as well as the judges and juries who are about to acquire these cases, to put a final stamp on justice." He slapped the table and stood up. "As Agent Miller said, go forth and heal this community. Rehabilitation from vice, of this degree, will take a long time. And I repeat, crimes of this type will never again happen under my watch. Meeting adjourned."

*****

Outside, on the steps of the Municipal Building, Lester Cranshaw and Mae Bolton observed the flutter of activity on Main Street. A 3 o'clock sun was shining in a cloudless sky. Each waited for the other to speak. At last, breathing a sigh of relief, they said in unison. "It's over."

Lester suddenly slapped the side of his trousers with his right hand, "By golly, I must tell you, Mae."

"It's something good, I hope," Mae blinked at him.

"I breezed in to see Topper before I came to this meeting." Lester looked pleased with himself. "It wasn't so bad after all. Topper's mind is quick... it's just the old body that's broken."

"Thank you, Lester." Mae looked at him smiling, her eyes very soft.

"And I promised the ol' gent I would bring him the paper on Tuesdays and, for fifteen minutes, read him the sports headlines." His face lit with pleasure. "I also told him I would bring Paddy with me as a care dog. Patches is too puppy rambunctious to bring along. Topper was beaming when I left."

Mae wrapped her arms around Lester and squeezed him tight. "Thank you, dear friend."

Awkwardly, Lester patted Mae on the back and gently pulled away, his cheeks colored red. "Where are you off to now, Mae?"

"I am going to drop a ham and potato casserole off to your house... it will be in the refrigerator; just heat it up in the oven for half an hour... and I'll drop one off to Cheryl Wilkes and the kids at Joyful Haven. The good news is they and Hopper will be moving into a new apartment next month. I will help them adjust. David will still work at Joyful Haven. How about you?"

"I'm off to my farm to feed Paddy and Patches and the animals. I want to check on our new hired hand, to see if Louis needs anything. He's done wonders at the farm already. And then I'm off to the cove, to say a rosary at the new chapel, with Caroline and Lily Moon. Maybe the Blessed Mother will appear to me." There was a sparkle in his eye.

"Amen." Mae blessed herself.

www.ingramcontent.com/pod-product-compliance
Lightning Source LLC
Chambersburg PA
CBHW020625250626
47154CB00004B/1668